Praise for Ellen Lesser's
The
OTHER WOMAN

"Ellen Lesser takes what would normally be a negative or stereo-typical figure, 'the other woman,' and allows her to mature before us. . . . This novel explores the underseams of relationships without any quick and easy answers. Lesser had my full attention from beginning to end."

—Jill McCorkle

"Thoughtful and provocative . . ."

—*St. Louis Post-Dispatch*

"There are few writers better able to describe the joy and heartbreak of love."

—W. D. Wetherell,
author of *The Man Who Loved Levittown*

"Lesser explores the end of a marriage and the beginning of a relationship with sensitivity that often has a humorous edge. She holds situations up to the reader to be seen in a new light. . . .*The Other Woman* is a complex tale, simply told by a promising author."

—*South Bend Tribune*

"Lesser has fashioned a wonderfully subtle portrait of the relationships between these characters . . . as gripping and dramatic in the way it unfolds as a mystery or a thriller . . . a novel of real drama and suspense, skillfully and even compellingly written—a first-rate story, full of wisdom and insight about human nature and relationships."

—Joyce Maynard, *Mademoiselle*

The
OTHER WOMAN

ELLEN LESSER

WASHINGTON SQUARE PRESS
PUBLISHED BY POCKET BOOKS
New York   London   Toronto   Sydney   Tokyo

The author gratefully acknowledges permission from the following sources to use lyrics from the works named:

"Hippopotamus Rock" from *RosenShontz Tickles You* © Rosen, Shontz, Kramer. Rosho Music, used by permission.

"Your Mother's Son-in-Law," written by Nichols & Holiner, copyright 1933, renewed 1961 Robbins Music Corporation. Rights assigned to SBK Catalogue Partnership. All rights controlled and administered by SBK Robbins Catalog Inc. International copyright secured. Made in USA. All rights reserved. Used by permission.

A Washington Square Press Publication of
POCKET BOOKS, a division of Simon & Schuster Inc.
1230 Avenue of the Americas, New York, NY 10020

ISBN: 0-671-66985-0

First Washington Square Press trade paperback printing June 1989

10 9 8 7 6 5 4 3 2 1

For their generous readership and suggestions, the author wishes to express her gratitude to Myra Lesser, Debbie Sontag, Geraldine North, Don Metz and Mary La Chapelle.

FOR ROGER

Part
One

CHAPTER 1

Jennifer ran around and made one final check of the farmhouse. Richard and the boy should have been here by now, but she was happy for the reprieve. The oatmeal cookies were cooling on her good china cake plate, up in the cabinet where Jet couldn't reach them. Jet's own bowl had been liberated of its usual slippery encrustation, his water dish fished clear of bloated, stray chunks of food. Earlier in the day she had vacuumed the whole place, but she could see as she passed through the living room and up the stairs a fine, dark down of Jet's hair settling over the floors again. But it didn't matter. It wasn't as if her mother were coming. Just a four-year-old boy. What would *he* care about dog hair? In the bedroom she found Jet in his usual spot: his broad, black muzzle on her pillow, his rear end on what was now Richard's. She sat on the bed, close enough to pull his head into her lap and rub the side of his nose. He groaned and stretched out his legs. "You lazy mutt," she said in her Jet singsong, and kissed the silky fur where his part-Labrador jowl became dewlap.

Jet had spent the whole day in bed. He didn't like housecleaning. He preferred anarchy, entropy, the happy abandon rooms could give way to when company wasn't expected.

"You've got to be good."

He slid over onto his back and half opened one eye.

"No stealing. No jumping up."

Jennifer not only hoped Jet would be good. She was counting on him to be the major attraction. As she'd cleaned, she'd scoured the rooms for something remotely resembling a toy, any object that might arouse a child's interest. There was the Russian box, with its miniature lacquered painting of some forgotten Slavic fairy tale. She was tempted to put that away—the boy might drop it or scratch it—but she told herself not to be miserly. There was her old set of Swiss colored pencils, and no shortage of paper. She had the nest of straw boxes, though those were really only a one- or two-shot affair. And then there was Jet, who could be a source of unending amusement if the boy took to him.

Jet stirred in her lap and let out a halfhearted *woof*. She listened, but it was just a car passing by. She slipped out from under the dog and went to the window anyway. What could be keeping them? She visualized the house she'd only seen from the outside, those few times she'd fallen prey to her curiosity and taken a slow, watchful drive through Richard's old neighborhood: that imposing, triple-story Victorian with its lofty pretensions and peeling porch. No doubt Ruth Ann had cornered him there when he'd gone to get Benjamin. Maybe Ruth Ann's therapist had given her a new way to conceptualize Richard's betrayal, her loss, and in the interest of keeping the channels open between them she'd be compelled to share the vision with Richard, so when he left to drive his first son to the new woman's house that acid guilt would turn like an extra engine inside him. Maybe he'd shown up just at the baby's feeding time, and the price of stealing a look at the little one would be to sit down next to Ruth Ann on the couch, to watch her unveil that swollen breast with a new self-consciousness that might even excite him. Sitting there with the two of them, might he not feel himself being drawn in, as by some inexorable force field at the center of that triangle: mother, father and child? Might he not stroke David's small cheek, tease the skin by the baby's mouth as it sucked, and feel almost as if he were touching her?

Downstairs again, Jennifer suddenly felt stupid for having baked the cookies. She'd have to avoid Richard's gaze when she trotted them out for Benjamin; she couldn't bear a look from him that acknowledged how hard she had tried. She took the plate down and rearranged the chunky circles until they looked casually stacked, then tasted one. It wasn't bad—it was her mother's old recipe —but would *he* like them? Benjamin. *Son of my right hand*—Richard had told her it meant that in Hebrew. She tried not to think about the time she'd met Benjamin (if you could call it that) but the image kept coming back: that perfect, sullen square of a face framed by the red of Richard's '66 Volvo.

She'd been crossing the street when Richard honked at her. She hadn't been thinking even remotely of him—it was back in the days when her occasional few hours with him were walled off from the rest of her life, when he was a pleasure she wanted to use and not get attached to— and so she was thrown by seeing him materialize there in his car, with the small boy up front beside him. She'd known he had two kids—Benjamin and David; the boy, the new baby—but still, actually seeing the child like that, she felt something turn hollow inside her. She came around and looked in at Richard from the passenger window; otherwise she'd have been standing in the middle of the street. The boy did not turn to look at her, and he seemed to give off a blue funk the way the Volvo did gas fumes. Richard said, "Benjamin, this is Jennifer," as if she were someone the boy were expecting to meet. Benjamin shot her a quick, grudging glance, devoid of curiosity, just long enough for her to ascertain that in spite of his humor the boy was beautiful, and looked nothing like Richard.

That night, for the first time, she found herself thinking about Richard in the way she figured *other women* must think. It was nine o'clock. She was sitting in bed with a mug of tea and a book but she wasn't reading or drinking. She was trying to imagine Richard at home with his wife and two children. No doubt the kids must be asleep by now. Were Richard and Ruth Ann doing something together? Jet was spreading his hair downstairs somewhere, or else in the guest room, tired of accommodating his sprawl to Jennifer's meager bulk in the bed, and so she felt alone, physically alone, to a degree she usually didn't. It was hard for her to imagine that Richard made love to his wife. The first time he'd been with Jennifer he'd devoured her in a way that could only bespeak a long hunger; his appetite had continued unabated through the two months of their affair, until she had to assume she was the only one feeding him. And yet she had no way of knowing for sure. Richard had never gone out of his way to avoid mentioning his wife, as in, "I'm building a new storage system for Ruth Ann's weaving studio," or, "I can't make that movie we talked about. Ruth Ann has a meeting at Benjamin's preschool." But he'd never said anything about *them,* how they got along, whether his stealing away from his office a couple of times a week to see Jennifer was any reflection on the health of his marriage.

She'd never asked, because to ask was to suggest that

she had some expectations. Up until that moment, she hadn't thought she had any. But now she had an unfamiliar, bitter taste in her mouth. The evening at home with her book and her tea suddenly wasn't enough. She wanted Richard there with her—Richard with his stories, his low, melodious voice; Richard with that woodsy musk of his she could almost conjure up as she sat there. She resented the other woman for having him.

She called out to Jet, but he only obeyed when he felt like it, and didn't come. She took a sip of her tea, almost cold now. She made a desperate visual tour of her bedroom: the collection of posters from New York museums, the recent card from her old college roommate, the maple rocker that had been her grandmother's. She pictured the wall of bookshelves in her office downstairs; the butcher block desk where she did her free-lance writing and editing projects and where, when she had the time and the nerve, she tried to write poetry; the cork panels over the desk, with the snapshots of her and her friends, her and Jet. She had a whole life that had been fine before *he* came into it. He was something extra, something that was only supposed to make her feel good. If she was going to start to brood, to feel jealous, she'd better get rid of him.

That had been in the spring, before the stormy summer that blew Richard out of the three-story Victorian and into her farmhouse on the outskirts of town, that led them to this September afternoon and her snitching cookies, waiting for him to come back with Benjamin. When Jet barked his way down the stairs to the door—he still hadn't gotten used to the sound of Richard's car in the driveway —she saw that through her reverie she'd snitched several, that the platter had taken on a sparser, less cornucopia look. She quickly spread the cookies out to conceal her indulgence, then rushed to catch a glimpse of herself in the bathroom mirror before they walked in. Her last cut was recent enough that the hair on top of her head still stood almost on end. She put some spit to the little tail growing out of the short hair in back; it was curling up waywardly. Her mother had told her this haircut made her look like a five-year-old boy. Maybe for today that would be a good thing. Maybe Benjamin would see her as some kind of new friend, and not make maternal comparisons.

It was a few minutes before they actually came in. Jet ran back and forth across the living room that also served as the entrance; he put his nose to the crack in the door, snorted and looked questioningly up at her. "It's okay," she said. "It's just Richard. And Benjamin."

When the door finally opened, she saw right off the reason for the delay: Benjamin was a vine that clung for all he was worth to his father's side. Jet, ever tactful, sniffed Benjamin's red corduroy bottom, then rooted in Richard's sweater for the boy's buried face. The sound that came forth was a garbled shriek, and then the blind hand struck out, connecting with the dog's face somewhere near the eye.

"Hey." She could see that Jet wasn't hurt, just surprised, but she looked up at Richard as though the affront to Jet's pride had somehow issued from *him*. "It's not the dog's fault."

Richard looked back at her, helpless in a way she hadn't seen him before. "Benjamin." The boy's face emerged from his father's side, as if to tally up the damage he had accomplished. Richard got down on one knee and held him out at arm's length. "You don't hit the dog. That's a nice dog."

Ben considered Jet for a moment through narrowed eyes: Jet, whose ears were already pitched up and forward,

16

whose tail was waiting for the slightest provocation to wag.

"You want to make friends with Jet?" Richard asked him.

The boy didn't nod, just looked with a widening of eyes at his father.

Richard put out a hand. Jet went over and sniffed it, then gave a tentative lick, as if awaiting further instructions. "Now you put yours out. Just like Papa."

Benjamin hesitated, but finally put out his small hand. Jet nosed it quickly, then went for the face, the disproportionate ear, only gently this time. Ben stepped back. Jet pursued. "Papa!" The voice was whiny but not without pleasure.

"Is he hurting you?"

"No. It tickles."

Richard laughed and Ben laughed, too, as he half offered his ear and neck, half pushed at Jet's muzzle. Richard looked up, to draw Jennifer into the game. She tried to keep her face neutral, even though it was hard to resist Richard's smile. She hadn't even been introduced (the time in the car didn't count); the boy hadn't so much as looked at her.

In a minute, Jet lost interest in the boy's scent, and pounced on a rubber hamburger. He paraded it around the room in his teeth, then collapsed in a noisy heap on the area rug and started to chew it.

"Papa, I'm thirsty," Ben said, and when Richard didn't respond right away: "I'm thirsty, Pop," with that whiny edge.

"Maybe you'd like to go into the kitchen with Jennifer and she'll get you some juice. You'd be happy to do that, wouldn't you, Jen?"

Richard winked at her, and for the first time since the

two had come in the door she remembered *they* were in this together, she and Richard, that the boy's behavior wasn't *his* doing. She gathered her face up into a smile, ready to lead the way toward the kitchen, the surprise of the cookies, which she was now grateful for.

Benjamin eyed her a second, but turned away with such a snap of his head, she might have been a witch, or some blinding abyss from an old moral fable. He reattached himself to his father's leg. "I want you to get it, Pop."

Richard shrugged and raised his eyebrows, but she had a harder time holding onto that conspiratorial feeling. She walked into the kitchen, pulled the cake platter down from the cabinet and set it out on the table with a peevish, *So there!* shove, as if it were out not because but in spite of Benjamin.

It must have been the cookies, Jennifer told herself, scraping the plateful of noodles and cheese sauce into the garbage bin. Benjamin had *said* the fettuccine was good —by dinnertime he'd warmed up enough that at least he was talking—though he'd hastened to add that his mother had a pasta machine, and usually served him homemade. It had been the same when he'd eaten the first of apparently too many cookies, and Jennifer had seen the change in his face, reluctantly won over by raisins, the hint of cinnamon, the stream of extra maple syrup that earlier she'd let slip from the jar. She was still watching him when he pulled himself up short, as though he'd just remembered an inner pact he'd made not to enjoy himself too much. "My mom makes oatmeal cookies, too," he said, slowing his eager attack to a nibble. "And peanut butter. Those are my favorite. When she has time."

Ruth Ann should have all the time in the world. Richard was in the process of making an unusually generous settlement, that would give her enough of his small-town lawyer's income to keep her in the Victorian house, to keep her from needing to find outside work until the baby was old enough to start preschool. The fact that Richard was giving away so much of his money didn't especially bother Jennifer. She'd been managing on her own, with only an occasional emergency dole from her parents, so whatever cash he could chip in each month was only a boon. Still, she wondered now and then how he'd have gotten along if he hadn't left Ruth Ann and the kids *for her*, but had just left them.

She stewed on that as she attacked the encrusted saucepot with renewed zeal. Her concentration was broken by a squeal from the living room, where Richard had been reading a chapter of *Peter Pan* but was now, from the sound of it, tickling Benjamin. The boy's laughter rumbled like an alien music above the running water, her stubborn steel wool. It was good Richard was having fun with his son; she'd known by the way he'd been brooding the last few days, by the skin of sadness over him even when they'd made love, that he needed this. And yet there was something in the sounds they were making— Benjamin's gasps and high, mock-desperate *Papas*, Richard's great, exploding brumskies, his rapid-fire rooster and turkey imitations—something in the sheer joy of them, that seemed somehow against her. She had to remind herself that Richard had told her to forget about dishes and come hear the story; that as she'd passed through on her way back from the bathroom, he'd reached across Benjamin and patted the empty spot on the couch. She was never one to wash dishes right after a meal, but tonight she'd clung to the specter of all that cheese turning hard and implacable, of Jet with his paws at the lip of the sink, rooting out any remains of what, next to meat, was his favorite substance. She was the one who had shut herself out, so why should she feel so rejected?

When she finished the dishes, she cleaned the counters and sink, listening to the wild tickling noises subside and the gentle tones of the story start up again. Finally she stopped wiping to zero in on the sounds—the repetitive, lulling melody beyond words of Richard's reading voice, the occasional counterpoint of Benjamin's tiny one with what must have been questions (*How did they do that, Papa? What does cavernous mean?*). She remembered the book her mother had read to her and her brother in bedtime installments when she couldn't have been much older than Benjamin. *Hans Brinker or The Silver Skates.* She could see the cover perfectly: its night-blue border and the old-fashioned illustration, the boy on his skates coming toward her out of the pond, the backdrop of windmill and countryside. Somehow the picture gave such an illusion of depth that looking at it, she'd always felt there really was a whole world there, and even now, though she'd forgotten the story, she had a memory of that fast slick of ice, the starlit Dutch sky, as if it were a place she had visited.

She took a quiet step toward the living room doorway, then stopped. Richard and Benjamin sat on the rug, their backs to the couch, the boy tucked so close in to his father's side he might have been nuzzling for warmth, or protection from some invisible danger. Jet was curled up on the couch, his head pointing past Benjamin's shoulder as if he were following the story. It was almost the perfect family scene except of course one person was missing, and there was something brave and sad about the two of them sitting there in her toyless, sparsely furnished living room, trying to pretend it was home, or that they were home enough for each other.

By the time Richard and Benjamin finished their chapter and came into the kitchen to find her, night had fallen and Benjamin's eyelids looked heavy with imagined adventure and sleep. "We've come to say good night," Richard said, and even he looked sleepy, as if he'd read himself into the same dreamy world where the boy was now floating.

"The room is all ready." She had a sudden, last-ditch desire to participate. "There are some extra towels—"

"It's okay." Richard put a hand over the boy's head, which was resting not far from his groin. "I'll give him his bath in the morning."

A mumbled sentence came from where the boy's face was buried. When Richard said, "What, Ben?" he spoke up more forcefully: "Will you carry me?"

"I'd be glad to. If you say good night to Jennifer and thank her for the nice dinner."

The *thanks* he threw out like a crumb wasn't much, but Richard raised his eyebrows to suggest it represented some kind of progress. He hoisted Benjamin onto his shoulder in what looked like a much-practiced motion. She called after them a hopeful good night that echoed and died in the spotless kitchen. Then she got Jet's leash from its hook by the door and led the dog out into the night.

The house was up the road from a dairy farm, and for the first quarter-mile of their walk, she and Jet were flanked on either side by cornfields, the stalks looming an eerie comfort over her head. She walked quickly, giving a series of sharp tugs on Jet's leash, hauling along the dog who wanted to linger, to sniff the ground for news of a hundred imperceptible voyages and transactions, to mete out his own few drops of scent on this sapling, that clump of ferns. She was after a sensation of motion, almost of flight, as if simply by walking she could transport herself beyond the reach of the house, the mysterious rituals being performed in her spare upstairs bedroom. As she walked, she remembered the night just about one month ago that she'd gotten the call from Richard. She hadn't been surprised to hear his voice at the other end of the line. He'd taken to doing that: leaving his house on the pretense of an evening stroll and ending up in the corner phone booth four blocks away, where he could talk to her about the various parts of her body he missed. But this time she knew by the silence after *It's me* that something was different.

"Richard?" Still there was just that dense static air. "Is anything wrong?"

He never said yes or no. He waited what seemed like a whole minute, and then said, "I told her."

At the end of the cornfield, the road took a dive, swooping down on the farmhouse and outbuildings' oasis of light. Jet paused like an approaching conqueror at the rise, nose high and testing the air for the pair of sheepdogs that usually kept their lackadaisical guard on the large farmhouse porch. She thought of turning back there, but he strained ahead on the leash and she followed him. When Richard said that, said *I told her*, she hadn't answered him. She was too torn between amazement and panic to figure out what to say. She'd known for a few weeks that this might be coming, ever since he'd taken her down to Boston to stay overnight. Yet she hadn't really believed it would happen; she certainly hadn't imagined it would happen so soon.

She'd been pleased, and a little shocked, at his plan for going to Boston: the fake alibi business trip, the dinner at the fancy Italian restaurant, the motel. Up until then there had been something safe and circumscribed about their infractions; they'd tucked themselves discreetly into the week, like the long, chatty lunch dates she sometimes allowed herself, the afternoon movies. They'd never required a specific *lie* to his wife, a dereliction of fatherly duties.

Jennifer had one friend Jet liked enough to stay with when Jennifer went away. Pat was fifteen years older than Jennifer, childless, long divorced. She'd been the only one of Jennifer's friends who wasn't aghast when she heard about Richard. Jennifer figured that for Pat, having been in and out of a marriage herself, the institution wasn't sacrosanct and untouchable the way it was for single friends her own age, young women who still saw marriage as something perfect and pure that lay waiting for them in their futures. But that morning when Jennifer dropped off Jet, Pat looked at her with a deep-etched furrow between her brows that reminded Jennifer of her mother. Probably she was a little worried herself; she could have let the look go and run off, but she hovered in Pat's kitchen, waiting for her to say something. She did: "Be careful." It was so simple and ominous, Jennifer wasn't sure how to answer. When she finally said, "I will," it came out sounding tentative; she'd realized in the moment she stood there that short of backing out of the trip —short of not seeing Richard at all—she no longer knew how to.

The Boston jaunt came off without the disaster Jennifer tried to watch out for. There were only two hitches. One was that spending the whole day and night and the better part of the next day together, they had enjoyed themselves too much, so by the time they found themselves back at her house, they could barely meet each other's eyes, for fear they would have to recognize what was beginning to look suspiciously like love. The other was that when Richard switched cars to go home (they'd taken her more able Honda to Boston) the Volvo was dead in her driveway.

At the bottom of the hill past the farmhouse, Jennifer came through a warm pocket of air, sweet with apples ripening in the invisible orchard, acrid from the cows that moved in the field like great, lumbering shadows. She stopped there. She wasn't ready to turn back, but she didn't want to walk on, up the next, sharp rise in the road. In her mind she was fixed on that picture of Richard: his arms draped over the steering wheel, his head down, when even the jumper cable transfusion didn't bring the car back to life. It wasn't then that he started talking, though. It was later, after he'd called a half-dozen garages and no one could come until the next day, after he'd called home several times and there was no answer. They could have gotten out of it easily enough. She could have driven him to within a block of his house; he could have fashioned a plausible tale of his breakdown, a friendly mechanic . . . But for some reason the mere brush with being found out pushed him over some edge, to where he had to complicate the lie by spending the night at her house so he could tell her all about him and Ruth Ann, and why he needed to leave her.

When Jennifer got back to the house, the light in the second bedroom was off, and she found herself wordlessly shushing Jet, his every movement thundered so in the silence. She made a pot of tea and got down two mugs, put it all on a tray and tiptoed up to the bedroom. She expected to find Richard reading in bed, but the room was empty, the covers unruffled. She stood there holding the tray a minute before it dawned on her: he must be in there with Benjamin. She set the tray down on the old wooden chest that served as a night table and went to the doorway of the spare room. Sure enough, the two of them were in bed. In the half-light from the hallway, Jennifer could make out Richard's form, stripped down to socks and boxer shorts, half covered by quilt, his arm reaching across the boy's hidden body. It was hard to tell if he'd just accidentally fallen asleep or if he'd been planning on spending the night there. She hesitated. Seeing him in the bed like that gave her the electric pulse with which her desire for him always started. She could probably wake him and help him out of there without waking Benjamin. But what if he didn't want her now? What if he'd wanted to sleep with his son?

Just then there was a sound in the bed that must have been Benjamin turning, and something spoken into the dark in a voice she scarcely recognized as the boy's. She couldn't tell for sure, but he might have said *bless you*, or *rescue*.

CHAPTER 2

It was the sound of a voice calling *Papa* that woke her. She didn't remember Benjamin right away. She'd been deep in a dream, a close variation on one of her standards: moving to a new place that always resembled the city where she'd gone to college, wandering the streets trying to figure out where one would go to meet some nice men. She'd been having this dream for several years now; being in a relationship didn't seem to make any difference. The difference came in waking up from the dream, the disorientation she felt when she reminded herself about Richard or Steven or Bob, the dawning relief that didn't quite cancel out the sense of panic, of emptiness, the dream always left her with.

The *Papa* sounded again, more insistent, and she placed Benjamin's voice, realized it came from the bathroom. Not only was she waking up to remember she did have a lover, a man in her life; now the awareness resurfacing took in the fact that she'd gotten a little boy in the bargain. There was one last, exasperated *Papa* and then Richard's footsteps. She heard a long, digestive gurgling

—water draining out of the tub—and after that, whispering, giggling, shushing. It was just as well that they left her alone, but still, she kept waiting for her door to swing open.

The clock on the night chest read seven-thirty. She wasn't sure what time she'd finally dropped off the night before, but she knew it was late. It wasn't that she couldn't sleep by herself. Richard had really scarcely moved in, and having the bed to herself (or herself and Jet) was more what she was used to. The problem was their *being there*, across the hall, in that other bedroom. Maybe Richard would wake up and come in to her. Maybe Benjamin would talk again in his sleep. She'd started to think of Ruth Ann, what the night must be like for her in her bedroom. Richard had told her how Ruth Ann had insisted on buying a king-sized bed, so she could sleep even farther away from him. Maybe she was happy to have it *all* to herself. But then there was her son, probably fine and asleep but not down the hall from her. Was Ruth Ann sitting up, wondering how it had gone at the farmhouse up on that hill across town? Wondering if her Ben had been nice to *that woman?*

Jennifer must have dozed off again. The next time she checked the clock, it was almost eight-thirty, and she knew by the weight of silence in the house that they'd gone. Down in the kitchen, a couple of plates and glasses sat rinsed in the sink, but there was no other sign of them. She felt certain Richard would have left her a note; she checked the kitchen, the living room, her desk, before giving up on it. She filled her coffee grinder with beans, pressed the button and enjoyed the rush of harsh sound. She told herself there was no reason to feel angry with Richard. What would the note have said, anyway, except what she already knew: *Taking Ben to school. See you here around six.* Maybe some routine endearment of the kind that still came hard to him, as if he were afraid that using those conventional niceties—the I-love-you's, the I'll-miss-you's—would make *them* conventional, domestic, routine, set them on the path of all the Ruth-Ann-and-Richards. What was it he'd said in Boston that night in the restaurant? He had not said, "I love you." He'd stopped eating and taken her hands across the table, one dancing spot of wine light on his cheek from some alchemy of chandelier and Chianti Classico. *There are things it's hard for me to tell someone.* That was it. From the look in his eyes she had naturally read the unspoken, carried away her own light from the moment as if he had actually *told her.* But now she found herself twisting the picture. She was an attractive woman with a house to herself and an income, and she wasn't Ruth Ann. From that angle it wasn't clear whether his glow had been entirely for *her* or for such a lovable circumstance.

The chemistry of love had always mystified Jennifer. It must have started out with her parents. They'd been married going on thirty years; on the surface one would expect that they'd have set a reassuring example. And yet for Jennifer, even as a young girl, the fact that her parents stayed together was as confounding as the separations rampant in their suburban town must have been for the kids who weren't so fortunate. How many nights had she lain awake behind the slender safety of her bedroom door, listening to what were not so much words as a furious music, complete with its crescendos of doors slamming, dishes shattering and finally the silence that was sometimes even worse than the noise. In the third grade she first heard of divorce; news had leaked out at the bus stop that Suzie Schiff's parents were getting one. The word took on a solid shape for Jennifer, became a dark talisman she carried sneaking into her brother's room on those nights. She'd push against the familiar lump in the bed if he wasn't already awake and whisper it: "Mommy and Daddy are going to get a divorce. I know they are."

Peter was only two years older than she. It wasn't that he was so much more mature but he liked to pretend to be, and part of that was accepting the ways of the adult world as if he had some inside information about them. He shoved at her until she got off his bed. "No, they're not. Don't be stupid."

She hissed her challenge out in the dark: "How do *you* know?"

"I just do. Now get out of here."

Peter of course had been right, and in a few years she would have a better idea about what had seemed from her side of the house to be the silence after the fights; their locked bedroom door when she got up in the morning; the look on her mother's face at breakfast, as if there really were such a thing as a *beauty sleep*, and once the yelling was over her mother had had one. Jennifer herself would jump, for her generation, late into sex, and as much as she liked it, part of her always distrusted it. It seemed to bring together people who'd have been better apart; others, its failure blinded to deeper compatibilities. She knew she and Richard had more between them than sex, yet sometimes it made her uneasy that the sex was so powerful. And of all the things Richard had told her about him and Ruth Ann, the fact that they barely ever made love was the thing she kept coming back to.

The day they'd driven home from Boston, Richard had slammed down the hood of the derelict Volvo and then hoisted himself up to sit on it, his legs dangling down over the grille in a way that made him look endearingly like a frustrated teenager. It was just dusk and the air was cooling nicely toward evening. Jennifer had called Pat, who was happy to keep Jet until the next day. Sooner or later Ruth Ann would be home to get Richard's phone call, his alibi. So Jennifer stood in front of him with a playful smirk tugging at the sides of her mouth, figuring the busted carburetor or alternator or distributor was a gift to them, an extra night they weren't audacious enough to take for themselves. There was no sense wasting the time they'd been granted on brooding, so she knelt down, craned her head sideways to see the face he was hiding. She got his attention, and gave him a teasing, *Come on, it will be okay* look. But his eyes turned back down quickly. "Sorry. I'm not in the mood."

She stood up and crossed her arms over her breasts, which she knew were plainly visible through her new Boston Aquarium T-shirt. It was as if she'd proposed sex and he'd turned her down, when that wasn't at all what she'd been proposing. "What kind of mood are you in, then?"

"I don't know." He didn't look up. He rested his running shoes on the fender. "I guess maybe I'm in the mood to talk about what the hell's going on."

Without saying anything more, they went inside and set themselves up on the couch with a bottle of wine, and Jennifer knew she was finally going to hear about Richard's marriage. Still, he didn't say anything for a long moment, and when he started, it was just to throw out one disjointed accusation after another, as if he'd never spoken about this to anyone, as if there were no logical place to begin.

Ruth Ann sat up every night reading these trashy biographies. She didn't like being outdoors. For all her feminist pretenses, she wouldn't lift a finger to change a light bulb or carry a piece of firewood. She saw a therapist twice every week, even though she claimed she didn't have any particular problems, and Richard never heard anything from her that hadn't already been talked out and analyzed and shaped into some neat little formula. She was always covering the refrigerator with lists and schedules and plans. She wasn't content only to map out her own life; she had to mastermind everyone else's.

Finally he slapped his hands down on his knees, as if he couldn't hope to explain. "The woman takes the life out of everything. Sometimes I feel like I'm going to suffocate. I walk into that house and I barely can breathe."

She poured herself more wine, and poured some for him, though his glass wasn't empty.

"If I left, she'd be bullshit. But not because she *loves* me."

"What do you mean?" The words *If I left* had startled her.

"I'm the husband. The father. The breadwinner. I'm part of her system." He took a long drink. "Do you know she never looks at me? I used to wear a beard. I shaved it off, and it took her a whole day to notice."

That's when she asked it: "Do you two make love?"

The way he looked at her, she was afraid for a second that she'd gone too far, stepped over some line of defense that still protected the heart of the marriage. But then he shrugged and laughed a sour little laugh. "You know what's amazing? At the beginning it was like that was all she wanted. Nonstop."

He stared into his wineglass, as if something were taking shape there. "It wasn't like anything *happened*, any one thing. It was gradual." He stopped, still reaching for something, and finally just said, "A lot can slide in eight years."

She twisted her mouth into a kind of false knowingness. Her longest relationship had lasted a year and a half. For her, eight years stretched out inconceivably.

"Sometimes I think it really went downhill when she got pregnant with Benjamin. But then I realize it started way before then. Right in the first year or so."

"So what was it?"

"Oh, you know. Her not wanting to. Not being in the mood. Sitting in bed with those fat biographies until I gave up and fell asleep. Jumping up and getting busy first thing in the morning. It literally got to the point where she didn't like me to touch her. Like if I touched her that meant I was hounding her. Like kissing your own wife is *pressure.*"

He paused just long enough to wet his throat with some wine; he was rolling now. "The thing was that when she wanted to—I mean, once a week, every two weeks—that was it. It might as well have been down on the calendar. We were doing it. I'd know because she'd be in the bathroom for ages and then she'd come out, all set with her diaphragm, this coconut lotion all over her thighs and her ass."

He stopped and sat back on the couch. She realized that the whole time he'd been talking, he hadn't looked at her, that he didn't look at her now. When he started up again, his voice sounded smaller, defeated. "I could handle all that. I mean, we still had our moments. We had Benjamin."

He took in and sighed out a deep breath, and she knew he had let something go, or that something had broken open.

"You know what finished it for me? I can pinpoint the exact moment. It was the weekend David got conceived. I was never sure about having the second baby. But she wanted to. That's all she talked about. She wasn't so young. I shouldn't make her wait like this. Finally I said what the hell. To get her off my back more than anything. So this one weekend we shipped Benjamin off. She got out the lingerie and massage oils and champagne. The whole business. And we had this marathon."

His mouth worked for a moment around what looked like disgust, as around a hard object.

"She was being so *sweet*. Trying to do all the things she figured I wanted. But it seemed wrong somehow. Like it was all calculated. Like even with the candles and music and everything, all I was doing was just plain *fucking* her. Fucking *my wife*. So that night I woke up at some point. She wasn't in bed, but I could tell she was standing there in the dark somewhere. I didn't move. I just waited. And then I heard this voice. It was like hers but it wasn't hers." He shook his head as though a shiver had come up through his spine. "It was so totally cold. So absolutely empty of anything. You know what she said? The great love of my life?"

She shook her head no.

" 'I hate your fucking guts.' "

He just spoke Ruth Ann's line, without any embellishment, and it hung, twisting and rank, in the air, the way it must have hung there that night. Then he looked into Jennifer's eyes, angry at the thought of Ruth Ann but sheepish toward Jennifer, as if asking a belated permission.

She took his hand but she didn't know what to say to him. She couldn't despise Ruth Ann for reading her glitzy biographies, for posting schedules, but she could despise her for *this*, she could feel that rescuing Richard had a kind of nobility. And yet part of her wished she hadn't heard it. Part of her wanted to roll the evening back, to watch the Volvo start up and carry Richard home to his life, however stifling. What did she want with a man who was in this sort of pain? What did she need with that kind of responsibility?

Richard told her that night that he wanted to leave Ruth Ann, but it wasn't anything definite, was only in some vague future when the baby was older, when *the time was right*. The next morning, Jennifer watched him ride off in the tow truck, the Volvo trailing behind like a dignified invalid. Then she went over to Pat's. "Don't get your hopes up," Pat told her. "These things drag on. It's amazing how hard it is to find the *right time* to leave a wife and two children."

Jennifer nodded. Pat of course thought she was delivering sobering news. Jennifer didn't want to admit that as much as she wanted Richard, the idea that he might never leave Ruth Ann could be a relief to her.

Only on the ride back from Pat's did Jennifer start to ponder the flip side of what Richard had told her—Ruth Ann's side. She had stayed at Pat's for an hour or so. They hadn't talked about Richard beyond their initial exchange. That was part of what she liked about Pat: she didn't sit around hashing out problems and relationships ad infinitum the way friends her own age did. She'd given Jennifer coffee and then brought her out into the garden, got her picking beans while Pat weeded and Jet sniffed his way along the wide beds of mulch between rows. By the time she went home, Jennifer felt calmer, normalized, centered back in a life that revolved around herself and Jet and her friendships with a few women. It was this crossing back over to the side of women that made her feel uncomfortable, traitorous, thinking about Ruth Ann. No doubt she would have her own ledger of small indignities, cumulative crimes; no doubt she had her reasons for what she'd become in her marriage to Richard. When had Jennifer ever pried into the secrets of someone else's sex life, except with her girlfriends? When had she ever taken the side of a man, telling tales about another woman?

That sense of tangled sympathies had lingered, and it came back to her now as she stared into her coffee mug. Of course Ruth Ann would never believe it. Just as she'd refused to believe that Jennifer wasn't the *reason* Richard had left, but only the thing he moved on to. As far as

Ruth Ann was concerned, Jennifer inhabited the absolute bottom of the moral order. She was a woman unsuited to be in the same house with Ruth Ann's first son, a woman definitely unfit to be handling her baby. She was a slut, a cunt, a faceless piece of fresh meat. She was just the kind of enemy Ruth Ann's righteous anger required—a person, by definition, incapable of any complexity.

None of this had been said right to Jennifer; she and Ruth Ann hadn't met or spoken or even bumped into each other since the trouble had started. She'd gotten it all out of Richard, evenings he'd come back to the house with that look as if his face had been taken apart and only partially put back together, and she knew he'd talked to Ruth Ann. "Tell me what she said," she insisted, and wouldn't let him alone till he did. "How bad could it be?"

It was always bad enough that she was left feeling sorry she'd pushed him. But Ruth Ann only thought those things because she didn't *know* Jennifer, because her grief demanded a scapegoat. The side of Jennifer that had always been the good girl clung stupidly to the conviction that Ruth Ann had only to meet her, to talk to her; that if Ruth Ann only gave her half a chance, she'd be swayed. Jennifer nursed a fantasy of running into Ruth Ann, of sending her a heart-melting, forthright, woman-to-woman gaze across their shopping bags and purses and those few feet of pavement.

The first time Jennifer had seen Ruth Ann was in Richard's office. She was writing a booklet for the Vermont Bar Association, traveling around to do a series of profiles of lawyers. That day she was in the office of Avery & Willis, to see Richard Avery. He'd gotten himself in the news several times for his environmental work, and she'd heard he was easy to talk to. She was glad. Her interview subjects for this project had been a dull lot; she'd saved Avery for near the end, so she'd have something to look forward to. But now she was sitting in his waiting room getting annoyed. She'd arrive at his office on time, which hadn't been easy; the roads were alternately sloppy and icy from a late winter storm. First his secretary had told her the lawyer was running behind schedule, and would be with her in about fifteen minutes. Fifteen was already turning to twenty when the woman walked in. The thing Jennifer would remember most clearly about her was that her coat was hanging open and she looked pregnant, even though Jennifer would later find out that the baby had been born four months earlier.

She had a bad feeling before the secretary even opened her mouth: "Good afternoon, Mrs. Avery. Was Mr. Avery expecting you?"

The lawyer's wife swept past the secretary's desk. "It's okay. I'll just be a minute." She knocked once and pushed open the door to the inner office.

It didn't take as long as Jennifer had feared. In a minute or two, the door opened. The woman came out with a triumphant look, as if she'd wrung some concession out of her husband—a look that stalled for a second at the sight of Jennifer, waiting there with her briefcase. But Jennifer never retained a precise image of Ruth Ann's face. She was too struck by Richard, who followed his wife out of the office—the way his yellow shirt brought out something almost gold in the depths of his eyes, the expression that was like a burner held by necessity down to a very low flame.

She had only seen Ruth Ann one other time, and then she hadn't quite *seen* her. It was a few weeks after the interview, and after a follow-up she always suspected was a pretext on Richard's part. This time he'd asked her to lunch, no excuses. She was happy to go. She'd gotten a naughty tingle as soon as she recognized his voice on the phone. Since their first meeting, he'd become a convenient object of fantasy. He was good-looking, she didn't know him, he had nothing to do with her life; it was too dangerous to daydream about someone that was a real possibility. And yet here he was, calling her, asking her to meet him at the café at twelve-thirty. She showered as if her body were a ritual object, being readied for offering. She dressed carefully in a loose sweater and not-so-loose jeans. She didn't begin to think about what it all really meant, to connect her own tingling with the woman she'd seen at the office.

She wasn't disappointed in that first lunch with Richard. She was only disappointed with herself, with what struck her by the middle of the meal as her own perversity. It was a perfectly straightforward lunch, between two adults who shared common interests. A couple of the environmental groups he was involved with might have some writing and editing work for her, if she had time. He wondered if she'd ever thought of going to work for a newspaper. What she'd studied in college. How she'd wound up in Vermont. Even after all her fanciful preparations, she wasn't sorry that it didn't seem to be about sex. That left her with a light-headed sense of relief, a feeling of being more, not less, of a person; after all, he was actually interested in *her*.

She was riding on that good mood, on a sense of possibilities opening, as she walked him back toward his office en route to her car. They were waiting by the light at the corner of Main Street and School Street when the brown Saab pulled up to the curb, and Richard leaned in to the window. She couldn't see in very well, though she did catch the head of long brown hair streaked with silver she recognized from the time in the office. That was the last time Richard had taken her to lunch at a restaurant right there in town. Apparently Ruth Ann was able to get a good look at *her*—good enough to ask him about her that night, good enough to store up an impression for later, when the young woman with the small breasts and no hips she had seen on the street corner would enter her life like a housebreaker.

When Jennifer finally stood up from the table, she wasn't sure if her stomach was sour from too much coffee, or from her thoughts. She needed to get out of the house, she knew that much. The catalog for the crafts guild wasn't due until the following week, and she was in no mood to write reverent paragraphs about handwoven shawls and luxury hardwood birdhouses. There was no way she could do her own writing. Paradoxically the poetry never seemed to go when she had something actual and burning to talk about. At those times she bogged down, got too literal. It only worked when her head was clear and she sat down at her desk with no particular idea in mind, as if just to play. That's when the deeper things came out, the things that surprised her.

When she was first seeing Richard, she'd written a lot— a few poems a week even. The structure of the affair left her a lot of free time, and seemed to give her a secret spring of energy. She didn't write about Richard, but just rode on the pleasure he gave her, the confidence, the long stories he told her as the lengthening May light found them in her bed after lovemaking—stories that tended to reach back into his boyhood to something pure and mischievous, beyond the constraints of respectability, of Ruth Ann. It always amazed her that he could remember his childhood so clearly, down to the first and last names of his comrades-in-arms, the precise reasoning behind their shenanigans. There was the time he and Joey Spencer set a vacant lot on fire, to clear the way for a traveling carnival; the hole he and Peter Benson cut in Peter's bedroom wall, so they could watch Peter's sister, Suzanne, when she went to the bathroom. Jennifer found herself thinking more about her own childhood, calling back things long forgotten and putting them into her poems. She wasn't sure the poems were any good, but she seemed to be worrying less about judging them.

Ever since the night she'd gotten *the call* from Richard, the "I told her" call—ever since he'd arrived with his collection of classical records and his single suitcase—the poems had stalled. It wasn't that she didn't have time. She had her weekdays free as usual, and for that first month Richard had been seeing his kids on the weekends—Saturday mornings taking care of the baby at the old house, while Ruth Ann did her shopping; Sunday taking Benjamin out for pancakes and a kids' matinee. Time wasn't the problem. It was that she felt herself sinking into an unfamiliar moral malaise. Richard leaving his wife wasn't her fault; she'd thought she was pretty clear about that. Without so much as thinking it out, she'd operated from the beginning on what she'd figured was a sound and ethical assumption: It was Richard's choice to see someone outside his marriage. That burden was his. Once he'd made his choice, she could act with him as with a free agent. All that was fine; it seemed perfectly reasonable. So why did she find herself thinking so much about Ruth Ann, and about what Ruth Ann thought of her?

She put away the milk, but left the rest of her coffee paraphernalia scattered. Upstairs, Jet was still lounging in bed. She clapped a hand down over his visible hindquarter. "Want to go out?" He jumped up instantly, like a doctor on call, and she fake-boxed the sides of his face with the flats of her hands. "You want to, don't you, boy? What's all this sitting and moping?"

While she tried to get dressed, Jet ran circles around her, slapped at her face with his tail, put his jaw around her stockinged foot and made like he was going to run off with it. Just when she'd gotten her sweatsuit and sneakers on, the phone rang. Probably Richard. She considered not answering, but decided she should. Maybe he wanted to apologize for last night, for the way he'd deserted her. She reached for the phone right at the third ring, all ready to sound nonchalant, not the least bit put-upon, but her "Hello" came out less confident than she'd have liked.

"Jennifer. It's your mother."

"Oh. Hi." She tried not to sound flustered. Her mother always announced herself with an ironical tone, as if she were someone you'd have never expected.

"Is anything wrong?"

"No. Everything's fine."

"Is this a bad time?"

"No. Not at all."

"You're sure?"

"Positive."

"Your father and I were just talking about you last night and I wanted to see how you were."

"I'm fine." She pronounced these two words with a studied conviction.

"How's the house?"

"Great. I'm supposed to get my firewood delivered tomorrow."

"And the dog?" Jennifer's mother never failed to inquire about Jet, the closest she had to a grandchild.

"He's fine, too."

"Good." Her mother paused then, as if she'd finally arrived at the brink of what she'd been leading to. She cleared her throat. "So. You been seeing anyone?"

Jennifer should have known. Wasn't this always ultimately the agenda? A bright, attractive young woman like you, up there alone in the woods—as if Vermont were a wasteland, a pioneer settlement. Jennifer didn't think it out. She just said, "Yeah, I am," and then stopped, sur-

prised at herself for giving in to expediency. But the lie—
or the truth—had already assumed its own momentum.
"Don't get all worked up about it, though. It's nothing
serious. I mean, it's just in a very preliminary stage."

"I'm not all worked up. I just want—your father and I
just want—for you to be happy."

"I'm happy, Mom."

"So who is he?"

Jennifer got a devilish urge. "Oh, he's just one of the
lawyers I interviewed." She could hear the pleased *Oh,
really?* in her mother's silence, imagine that look of de-
spicable hope on her face. Why was Jennifer doing this?
She found herself scrambling, and figured it served her
right. "Let's not talk about it now, okay? Like I said, it's
just in sort of a trial period."

"Sure, I understand."

Like hell she did.

"Maybe when we come up to see you one of these days
we can take the young man out to dinner."

The young man: Richard was practically forty. "If I'm
still seeing him."

"Don't say that. You've got to think positively about
these things. You never know."

"Okay. I'll think positively, Mom." Jennifer had
brought this on herself, so she had to humor her mother.
Even at her age, Marilyn Gold was a hopeless romantic.
"You never know" was short for, "You never know, this
may be the one"—as if every daughter had an exclusive
match waiting for her somewhere out there, and had only
to find him.

Instead of striking out down the road, Jennifer cut
through the backyard to the woods, where a narrow trail
led to a broader logging road that snaked back up the
mountain. She wanted the strenuous climb. She couldn't

believe herself. What softhearted, shortsighted desire to please had made her say those things to her mother? Now there would be no end of sly phone calls, of questions. If her mother—her upright, monogamous mother—only knew half the truth of it.

Jennifer had connected up to the main trail; the climb was getting steeper. Every couple of minutes Jet appeared above her and watched her catch up. "Good boy," she called out. "Good trail dog." But her voice lacked the exuberance, the abandon, she usually felt with Jet in the woods. She pushed herself to walk faster and tried to empty her head, to concentrate on long, steady breaths and her heart pounding.

All around her the trees were inching toward autumn; at every turn in the trail, maples sent out bright shots of crimson like warning flares. Maybe the biggest lie she'd told her mother was that she was happy. She wasn't. At least not today. She'd been hard-nosed about her own happiness when the affair with Richard was just an *affair*. She'd always been hard-nosed about her own happiness. She'd wanted to live in the country, so she'd moved to Vermont, in spite of the outcry from friends and family. She wanted to be her own boss, to try to write poetry, so she'd bullied herself into a free-lance business. And she'd been hard-nosed about relationships. She'd never understood her friends, who stayed on and on with guys who were plainly destroying them. When things started to turn the least bit sour, she always got out. Maybe things were starting to go sour now with Richard. Not Richard himself, but all the baggage that came along with him.

The day he'd moved in, he'd no sooner gotten his suitcase inside the door than the phone rang. Jennifer answered it. "Would you put my husband on the telephone, please." Not Richard. *My husband.*

Jennifer handed the phone to him. She thought about

leaving the room, but he wasn't saying anything. He held the receiver a couple of inches away from his ear, so she was party to the harangue—at least the rhythms and tone of it. She was pretty sure she heard Benjamin's name several times, something about the boy wetting his bed. Finally Richard said, "Put him on. I want to talk to him."

He turned his back to her while he waited. "Benjamin? Benny Boy, this is Papa. Talk a little louder, okay, sweetheart?"

While he listened, his body seemed to curl inward, deflate.

"No, Ben. Papa loves you and David. You're still my good boys, okay? You'll never stop being my boys."

When he hung up, he took a moment before he turned back around to her. There was something naked and terrible about his face just then, and she was sure it wasn't only a trick of the light, that slick place over his cheekbones. Her own face must have betrayed something she'd rather have kept hidden, because he said, "Can you handle it?"

Before she expected to, Jennifer found herself nearing the top of the hill, the blue light slashing in among the sparse birches. She stopped. When the pounding of blood in her ears had subsided, she listened. There was a road not far from the hill down below, but the whoosh of cars became one with the wind, the way—from this height— all the little sounds of the world blended and receded into one surrounding, benevolent whisper. Jet came trotting smartly out of the brush, and nuzzled into her knees. Maybe she'd stay up here all day. What if she *couldn't* handle it?

CHAPTER 3

After Benjamin's visit, Ruth Ann didn't call or appear at Richard's office for a couple of days. It was a lull in hostilities that Jennifer mistrusted but relished anyway— a lull she needed to separate her and Richard from the shrapnel of his exploded family. She decided to surprise him with a romantic dinner at home; she kicked off work early and drove into town, to pick up what she needed. Unlike Ruth Ann, she was no gourmet cook, but she could sauté shrimp in lemon and garlic, heat up French bread, set a table with wine and the battered elegance of brass candlesticks her great-grandmother had carried over on the boat for a dowry. She went into a small shop that sold cards and gifts, and stood for a long, wasteful moment in front of a rack of flawless, hand-dipped tapers in every imaginable hue. She finally chose a pair in the deepest night blue, and left the shop with a vision of them presiding over her blue-and-white tablecloth. She thought of all the nights she'd been living alone, grabbing a bagel here, a piece of fruit there, barely bothering to sit down at the table. Before Richard moved in, she'd never once cooked for him, never done more than offer him coffee. They'd spent the little time they'd had talking and making love; they hadn't wasted it on something so mundane as eating. But now the simple domestic rites—the meals, the baths, the reading in bed—took on an exotic sexual aura. It was those very things, after all, that during their illicit affair had been the most unattainable.

She was musing along these lines, adjusting her grasp on the array of small bags, when she saw her. She had to stop and stare for a moment, because at first glance she wasn't positive it was really Ruth Ann. Then she realized the difference. The hair that had been graying brown was now a lustrous auburn, and shorter: a sharp curtain that fell down the cheek and ended bluntly, perfectly, just above the line of the shoulders. Jennifer didn't get much time to consider the face, and she didn't have a very clear image from the past to compare it to, and yet it would strike her, once Ruth Ann had passed by, that something was different there also—brighter, better defined; that Ruth Ann, whose face that day in the office had been unadorned like Jennifer's own, was now wearing makeup. Ruth Ann was toward the outer edge of the sidewalk, and Jennifer had stopped frozen close to a store window. Was it possible that Ruth Ann hadn't noticed her? Or had she spotted her in advance, and steeled herself to make a show of not noticing?

Jennifer got a grip on her packages and pushed herself up the street with a wary look backward, just in time to see that flawlessly shaped, tinted head disappear round a corner. She stopped again and kept looking that way, as at some shimmering afterimage. The hairdo and makeup had to be brand-new. In fact, Ruth Ann had probably just left the salon: she'd carried herself as if she were afraid to let a strand slip out of place, as if she were worried her face might break.

Jennifer forgot to stop for the ice cream she'd planned for dessert. As she drove home, she found herself admitting there was a kind of hard beauty to the artifice of Ruth Ann's new look. But that wasn't what bothered her; she had no need to be jealous of Ruth Ann's appearance. What disturbed her was the idea that Ruth Ann could change like that, the sense that Ruth Ann's changes were somehow a menace to her own life.

Back home, she went through the motions of preparing the dinner, cleaning the veins of excrement from the shrimp the way she might excise a dark channel out of her evening, laughing a mean, inward laugh at the perfect sanctity of her table-for-two. It was as if there were an invisible third place set, and Ruth Ann, new hairdo and all, would be there in the room with them. But when Richard came in he was charmed by the table, the optimistic wax columns, the blue. He dipped her back in his arms like some expert ballroom dancer, kissed her hard on the mouth. Obviously he hadn't seen Ruth Ann, hadn't talked to her; his face looked like the face of the man who'd come into her house on those mornings in spring.

The part of her that was still stopped, jaw slack, on the sidewalk, knew Ruth Ann's silence was only a gathering of forces toward some new offensive. But she could keep that news to herself. Richard was whispering something into her ear—it might have been only her name—and reaching under the sweatshirt she hadn't gotten a chance to change out of. And couldn't it be just the two of them for this evening? He was touching her now, but she wouldn't touch him yet. She would stand there a minute and feel the way her skin turned to gooseflesh beneath his smart fingers, this power that would never again be Ruth Ann's.

•　　•　　•

When Jennifer and Richard made love, she tried to keep her eyes always open, so she'd know it was him—him and not just anyone giving her pleasure. Something had happened to her the first time she'd done that—maybe the third or fourth time they'd made love—something even better than the pleasure itself. She had never explained it to anyone, even to Richard, and in her own mind she had no words for it, only a picture: his face when she was looking into it, coming, until it became not an object but the natural curve of her gaze, until there was such a symbiosis of pleasure in pleasure on their two faces, that in seeing his she was seeing her own, simultaneously seeing both of them. She realized that once you'd seen someone's face like that, it would always look different. When she'd first met him, she'd thought he was handsome: the soulful hollows beneath the brown-and-gold eyes, the strong line of his nose, the full lips that were almost feminine. But she didn't see these things anymore, as separate, objectifiable features. She didn't look at him and think, *handsome*. She only looked and saw the man who made love to her, who reflected her back so beautifully to herself.

"You think I'll still be able to get it up when I'm seventy?"

She laughed. "What the hell are you talking about?"

He was lying on his back, twirling ringlets of chest hair around an index finger, in the dreamy way he had after sex sometimes. They'd eaten dinner, finished the bottle of wine, watched the blue wax icicle down over the lips of the candlesticks. "When I'm seventy, you'll be fifty-eight."

That was true. There was twelve years' difference. "So?" She left her nest down by his hip and leaned up on her elbows to look at him.

"So." He got a devious look in his eye, like a kid about to pronounce a bad word. "Will you still suck on it?"

She laughed again, and slid her elbows down over the mattress. "No way."

"Why not?" He poked a finger into her rib cage.

"Because." She hugged her arms around herself as if for protection.

The finger found a spot behind her ear, and one near her armpit. "Because why?"

"Because," she repeated, and it almost came to her lips: "Who says when you're seventy we'll still be together?" But she didn't say that, probably couldn't have, because now he was tickling in earnest, she was struggling and crying out, until Jet came running, nose into the fray. "That's right. Save me, boy."

Richard stopped tickling, and held her tight around the waist, her back and buttocks hard against him. When she caught her breath, she said, "Who do you think I am? Benjamin?" She was instantly sorry, because he didn't answer, and tightened his grip. She didn't have to turn around to know his face had gone wistful.

He held on, not speaking, his breath slowing and dwindling against her neck until she figured he must be asleep. But she would never sleep like that; he had her in a grip like a vise. She worked to loosen his arms without waking him. After a minute he shifted and turned with a sigh that didn't sound like contentment. She could tell by the light out the small window a moon was up, and part of her wanted to creep up and dress, to go walking. But she stayed, watching him, and thought for the first time in a couple of hours of Ruth Ann. She still couldn't fathom how a woman who'd loved a man enough to marry him, to have kids with him, could arrive at those words in the night—how what started out so fine and hopeful could turn like that.

She'd seen love turn in her own life, of course, but there was a difference; before this she'd never met anyone she'd have remotely considered *marrying*. In every guy she'd ever gone out with, she'd perceived from the start certain shortfalls, what would become fatal flaws—timebombs ticking at the heart of a transient relationship. She'd known Steve was threatened by the idea of her writing poetry, her reading books he couldn't understand and so felt compelled to make fun of. Bob was sweet, but he loved her too much, with a solicitude that was finally sickening. Gerry wasn't much of a talker, and there were his cigarettes; she could only tolerate smoke for so many months—smoke in her hair, in her underclothes.

That was the thing about Richard: On an obvious level, he had come to her flawed, a man with the handicap of a family. But forgetting the baggage, thinking only of Richard himself, there was nothing about him that bothered her, nothing that made her figure she was just biding her time. She couldn't foresee their downfall, the way she'd more or less foreseen all the others. And what that left was an open question, a strangely undelimited space, which could even mean she'd be with him when he was seventy, eighty. Or it could simply mean she wouldn't know the end in advance this time—the small irritations that would start surfacing, the resentments, the distances. It could mean that for the first time she was taking a chance.

Jennifer wanted to keep distracting Richard from Ruth Ann and the kids; the next morning she proposed that they meet after work at Villa Alfredo. She arrived a bit early and got a table, ordered a bottle of wine. From her vantage point she had plenty of time to consider his progress across the expanse of converted barn that was the restaurant's dining room. He didn't look quite like himself. He had a charge around him, as if he'd witnessed an accident or a roadside miracle. He took the seat across from her and leaned forward. "We've got to talk." He said this with a pointed intensity, as if to talk would require making some other arrangements.

She took a sip of the wine, the same Chianti Richard had ordered in Boston. She was working to formulate some smart crack about setting a secret rendezvous when she looked at his face again, and knew, or thought she knew in that moment: he was deadly serious; he was going back to them. She swallowed hard on the end of the wine, that smooth and suddenly regrettable aftertaste. "Okay."

The waiter arrived just then with his viciously detailed recital of specials. She kept her eyes on him to avoid looking at Richard. He was a young man, probably her age, maybe younger. He had inviting, almost-green eyes, and she fixed on them as on an escape hatch. Stuffed loin of veal with prosciutto and spinach and fresh mozzarella. She nodded, as if she could care less about food. He was speaking the dishes right into her eyes now, practically ignoring Richard, and she held his gaze through the last sauce and accompaniment, but casually, casually. If Richard said he was going back, she'd be cool. There were other men out there who didn't have such tangled strings. There were men with whom her life would be simpler.

They ordered according to what had become their usual practice: two appetizers, two entrées, which they would go on to split. She thought there was something perverse in this, if she was right in reading what was to come. She dug into the basket and pulled off a big hunk of bread, though she was no longer hungry. She thanked the waiter, who might have gotten embarrassed by her look, he fled the table so quickly. "So," she said.

"So. Ruth Ann called today."

Of course. "And?"

"And it looks like we're coming into some changes."

"We?"

He gave her a funny look. "Yeah. We. Assuming you're still part of this."

She bit down on the bread to buy herself time. She studied *his* eyes now, the gold depths that shone even in this dim light, and realized she had misread him. She tried to swallow too soon, and took a moment to get her voice back. "I hope so."

"Then what are we talking about?"

"You tell me."

"Ruth Ann called today."

"You said that already."

Ruth Ann had called to say that the most important thing was that she and Richard stay on reasonable terms for the sake of the children. She'd also decided it was time Richard started seeing more of the boys. David was eight months old, and she was starting to wean him. She thought that in a couple of weeks, Richard could start taking him for a night here and there. Then, in a month or so, Richard could take both boys for the weekends.

"The weekends?" She took a sip of wine to maintain an air of neutrality. "Like the whole thing?"

"I'd get them Friday afternoon and bring them back Sunday." The way he pronounced this, she realized that for him it was not an imposition but a triumph, a luxury.

"Every week." She didn't bother phrasing this as a question.

He nodded. "More or less. As long as it's okay with you."

She balled up a morsel of bread and stared at it. *Okay with her.* And what, she didn't dare ask, if it wasn't? The rigor of the arrangement, its finality, daunted her; it was just like Ruth Ann's famous schedules and lists, the way it mapped everything out, irrevocably, into the future. "Does it have to be only the weekends? I mean, couldn't you alternate, like sometimes—"

He cut in. Ruth Ann was pretty firm on the weekend point. Jennifer thought she could hear her in the phrases he parroted, and behind that, her therapist: Ruth Ann was suddenly, unexpectedly, in the position of having to rebuild a social life. If she had any hopes of getting out and meeting people, she needed her weekends. Jennifer and Richard had each other already. They could go out whenever they wanted. Saturday, Tuesday: what did it matter to them?

"I see." Jennifer knew she was stalling the inevitable, *it's okay.* She wanted to ask Richard how he thought Ruth Ann would make out in the bars, but decided he might not think that was funny. Then she remembered the haircut. She held her tongue for the moment, because the waiter arrived with the mussels, the roasted peppers and anchovies. She barely met his eye this time, and felt deliciously fickle. When he left, she came out with it: "I saw Ruth Ann in town yesterday." She paused to maximize her effect. "She's gotten herself a make-over," leaning heavily on the last word, to conjure up a kind of beauty magazine triviality.

"I know."

"You know?"

"She came in today. To the office."

"I thought she *called.*"

"She called. Then she came in."

She nodded and took a stab at a pepper. This didn't matter, whether she called or came in. It wasn't as if he were trying to hide something. "So what do you think?"

"What do I think? I hate all that shit. The makeup. That goddamn hair color. I can't believe she thinks it's attractive. Mind you, this is a woman who'll only let health food into the house. Who makes a big deal about using only natural vegetable dyes for her weavings."

She allowed herself a tight smile; here was one small point she was winning over Ruth Ann, even as the woman was muscling further into her life, into the life she was hoping to carve out with Richard. But there was something in the venom of Richard's distaste—the fact that he could take it so personally, that for a long time he'd probably be capable of taking anything Ruth Ann did personally. "At least you don't have to live with it."

"Amen." He toasted the sentiment with half a mussel shell full of broth. "I'll tell you what gets me. When we were together she didn't do shit for herself. And I'm not talking makeup. I'm talking basic things. Like her body." He lowered his voice and leaned forward over the mussels, as if somebody might overhear. "Do you know when she was pregnant with David, she gained sixty pounds? She just ate her way through it. I tried to tell her. *Remember how good you were with Benjamin? Remember what it was like after, trying to get yourself back?* The more I said anything, the more she kept stuffing herself. Like I swear she was going out of her way to be as repulsive as possible."

He pushed the mussels over to her side of the table, though he hadn't eaten nearly his share.

"So afterward she got this thing. Some women get it." He pushed his chair back a little and laid his hands over his abdomen. "It's like all the muscles down there *give out.*"

She couldn't picture it, but she didn't want to. She was trying to eat; she was still far enough from any interest in motherhood that the explicit, physical subject of pregnancy, of childbirth, made her squeamish.

He looked as if he were going to say more on the subject, but then saw the expression on her face. "Anyway.

Now she tells me she's joined Fit for Life. You know, that fancy health club up on Ridge Terrace. She tells me she's lost ten pounds in three weeks. You've got to see the look on her face when she says it. The same *fuck you* look she used to get when she'd tell me she'd exercise if she felt like it." He poked his fork at an anchovy, embarrassed suddenly, as if the heat in his voice were an admission he hadn't wanted to make.

"Anyway." She tried to save him. "The baby. Weekends."

"Yeah, right. And one more thing."

"What's that?"

"She's going to call you."

"Call *me*?"

"She wants you to come to the house. To have a little talk with her."

"She wants to make friends?" She guarded her voice with a mockery of hope. "Tea and cookies?"

"I don't think that's quite what she has in mind."

"Oh. Too bad."

"Listen, I told her I don't want you to go. She said I should let you make that decision."

"What do you think she's going to say?"

"I don't know." Richard pushed his plate to the side. "She wouldn't tell me. She says it's between the two of you. All I know is I don't want you going there."

There was something so dramatic about the look in his eyes, the sinister arc of his eyebrows, she had to stifle a laugh. "You make it sound like she's going to get me there and then murder me."

He wasn't amused. "I wouldn't put anything past her."

Ruth Ann didn't call until the next afternoon, so Jennifer had plenty of time to imagine and reimagine the conversation, to plan what she'd say. One thing she knew from the start was that she was going to go, no matter what Richard wanted. Not to go struck her as an admission of guilt, or at least an admission of weakness. She wasn't ashamed of who she was, or what she had done; she wasn't afraid to show herself. That was the reason she gave Richard at breakfast. "I can't *not go*."

He was at the table drinking his one cup of coffee. She was already onto her second and couldn't sit still. She was hovering over him, as if it were crucial that he be convinced, that he send her forth with his blessing.

"Bullshit. You don't have to prove anything to her."

"It's not so much *that*." She said it but she wasn't so sure. She drank some more coffee, though that wasn't helping. Probably she did hope to make some kind of statement by going. And maybe she needed to prove this thing—her integrity or whatever it was—as much to herself as to the other woman.

She didn't say that, though. She switched arguments. "A lot of it is just curiosity." There was some truth in this. She wanted to hear what Ruth Ann would say—the same way she'd pestered Richard for her secondhand insults. She wanted to see the inside of the house. She wanted to see Ruth Ann herself—how she talked, how she moved, what her face really looked like. Jennifer phrased it in a way that was more casual than her actual interest. "You know. I want to check her out."

"You want me to get you some photographs?"

"Come on. I'm serious."

"So am I."

He stood up and took her face in both hands, planted a kiss on each eyelid, at the bridge of her nose. That whisper touch of his lips imparted a calm that had nothing to do with how she felt right now, but she stayed inside of it for a moment before he let her face go, and for a moment after that.

She followed him out through the living room, out the door, even though the morning was too cool for her T-shirt, her stockinged feet. She stood hugging herself at the edge of the slate path some former occupant had laid with more whimsy than skill. Her standing there had the effect of a question, though she didn't say anything.

He spoke across the roof of the Volvo. "Do what you want."

"You think?"

"Just remember she likes to control people. The more the merrier."

When he drove off, she hobbled back across the cold stones to the door, where she found Jet waiting. "She doesn't control me," she said to the dog. "She doesn't control my boy." But when he pushed at the leash with his nose and looked at the door, she had to say no. "We can't go now. I've got a phone call to wait for."

CHAPTER 4

Part of her was able to notice the trees, the way it wasn't only the maples turning now, but whole hillsides. But over them or through them like a double exposure she saw Richard's face, how he kept looking and looking at her before he drove off that morning, as if the next time he saw her she'd be irrevocably changed. And though she was listening to a tape of Mozart, his Mozart, what she was hearing was that voice on the telephone. "Hello. This is Ruth Ann Avery." *His name.*

She had been ready for Ruth Ann, but that threw her, and she had to swallow before she could speak. "Hi. Richard said you'd be calling."

"He probably also said you shouldn't come talk to me." What was it in her voice? A trace of condescension, as if Jennifer were a child and Ruth Ann the mother or teacher, coaxing but underneath needling, stern.

"No. I have every intention of coming. I'm looking forward to the opportunity." When she'd planned it out, there had been more than that—something about the two of them coming to an understanding—but she stalled.

"Yes, I'm sure." Ruth Ann's voice fairly dripped with disdain. "Tomorrow at one o'clock suit you?"

Now it was ten before one, and Jennifer could see already she was going to be early. Still, she continued on through the middle of town toward the neighborhood of Victorian houses, of families, of plastic scooters and tricycles parked in driveways like serious vehicles. Richard had asked why they couldn't meet on neutral turf, and though she'd insisted the place didn't matter, she could see his point now. Wasn't there a kind of moral authority emanating from the very neighborhood, the beds of perennial flowers, the weed-free, smartly mown lawns?

She pulled over in front of a house with a meticulous, three-color paint job, a block down from Ruth Ann's place. How did people live inside perfect, storybook houses like this? Were they happy? The domestic fireworks of her own childhood home had always found an external expression in monstrous piles of trash left out by the curb like ejected relatives, in highly visible and eternally unfinished carpentry, in rusting garden equipment, in newspapers that had sat out so long they'd sogged and faded to a uniform, illegible gray. *Her* mother never would have been caught whispering a secret hatred into the dark bedroom air. Her mother didn't whisper, she shouted.

At a few minutes to one, Jennifer pulled slowly upward the house, in time to see Ruth Ann on the porch, passing a bundle shaped like a baby into another woman's arms. The two stood and spoke for a moment, and then Ruth Ann disappeared back through the door. Jennifer waited in her car one house down until the woman strapped the invisible David into a car seat, drove off. So the place had been cleared. It would be only she and Ruth Ann, one on one, but with the implied shadow of family falling and lengthening around them.

She turned off the car and locked all the doors, though she normally wouldn't, midday, on a street like this. She didn't want to appear to be stalling, though; she felt watched, as if Ruth Ann were there at one of the windows. But probably it was only her own sudden self-consciousness. She'd dressed neatly but down, in jeans, a corduroy shirt and high-top basketball sneakers, no makeup or jewelry: the kind of young woman who lives in a farmhouse and has a big dog and stacks wood, who'd never intentionally break up someone's family. Now, pausing before she took her first step up to the porch, she wished she'd done something to make herself look a bit older; wished she'd gone a less woodsy, more professional route. Looking at the three stories, intact and looming over her, she would have given anything for a briefcase or blazer or purse—any prop for her dignity.

Of course Ruth Ann must have known she'd arrived. Another territorial prerogative: the woman of the house would make the visitor ring the bell, make her stand there. Benjamin had a molded plastic slide and a big-wheeled tricycle on the porch. There was a basket for mail hanging right by the buzzer, which she pushed again, a bill from Ener-G Natural Gas addressed to Mr. Richard Avery. The footsteps fell in measured beats across what must have been a long hallway, and she swallowed quickly, throat tight. This chemical panic had nothing to do with integrity.

Ruth Ann's hair was clipped back in two simple plastic barrettes, and she'd left off all but a trace of her makeup. Obviously, for this occasion, she hadn't intended to look especially glamorous. In the rush of light through the door, Jennifer could see the tiny lines like patterns of flight moving out from her eyes, the etched memory of a smile even within this grim countenance. There was something Slavic and comforting about the low, broad sweep of her forehead, the wide, squared-off jaw, and for an instant Jennifer imagined what it would be like to have this face as a mother's face, to have it smiling and bending over you.

Ruth Ann did not say hello. "You can take your shoes off and leave them here on the mat," she said.

Jennifer hesitated a moment before she bent down to her laces. Her sneakers were perfectly clean; they weren't about to track up Ruth Ann's precious parquet. But the woman stood there staring her down, as if to ask what she was waiting for. Even as Jennifer knelt, she felt that she was conceding some small but critical point. Maybe Richard had been right after all. Maybe she'd conceded a point by the simple fact of being there.

Ruth Ann was a little taller than Jennifer, with a much fuller, more womanly figure, discernible even beneath the overlarge shirt she was wearing, a shirt that looked suspiciously like one of Richard's old oxford-cloth button-downs. Jennifer followed her down the hallway, hung on either side with weavings that must have been Ruth Ann's own, large, somber fabrics of evergreens and browns, spiked here and there with dried flowers or feathers. She followed her into a living room with no furniture—just a couple of pillows on a bare wooden floor. Jennifer remembered the day a few weeks ago Richard had come home in an uproar because Ruth Ann was selling all their furniture and rugs at a yard sale, where she couldn't hope to get very much, and was going to redecorate—now of all times, when money would be getting tighter. Yet Ruth Ann stood in the middle of the barren room like a woman bereft, as if Jennifer had not only taken the husband out from under her, but the coffee table, the couch.

"You'll have to just sit on the floor, or take one of the cushions," she said with a resigned look, as though she were beginning to make her peace with the poverty of these offerings. From the corner by the window she pulled up something Jennifer hadn't noticed—a child-sized wooden chair, painted a playroom blue and dotted with faded teddy-bear decals. She set it up across from where Jennifer had perched uncertainly on a pillow, with that same trumped-up, I-make-do-with-what's-left-to-me look. When she sat down, her bottom extended out on either side beyond the chair's edges.

Taking in the sight of Ruth Ann, the exquisite calculation of her undersized throne, it never occurred to Jennifer to say, "So. When's your new living room furniture coming?" That would be only one of the lines she'd pronounce flawlessly in her head with the bitter relish of lost opportunity, later that day and that night, and in the weeks that would follow.

Ruth Ann sat on the kiddie chair for a minute without saying anything. She was holding a yellow legal pad in her lap—the kind Richard brought home from his office. Her eyes were on the pad, and when she finally looked up at Jennifer, her face had a grim, deliberate set. "I don't want you to imagine that this is easy for me—sitting across from you in my home, the home where I've tried to conduct a marriage and raise a family."

Jennifer had the curious sensation that she was not being *spoken to*, and almost in the same instant she understood why. Ruth Ann *wasn't* talking. She was reading from the yellow pad. Jennifer saw it all in a flash: Ruth Ann writing out her remarks, then checking them through with her therapist. Or Ruth Ann and the therapist in the therapist's office, composing the sermon together. Ruth Ann's lists and agendas, her need for control —to control this, of all conversations.

"But there are certain things that you need to hear, and that I need to say to you."

"Listen. I see you've got all this stuff written out. But can't we just—"

"Excuse me." Ruth Ann looked back to the pad, as if she had a response prepared for just this interruption. "I know this may be uncomfortable for you, in your position." She looked up at Jennifer and looked through her, as if there were an image—a target—posted on the wall behind Jennifer's head. "But given what you've taken from me, I think you owe me at least the consideration of listening."

Yes, she was reading this, too. It was all written down there. "I'm sorry, but I think you're making some assumptions I don't necessarily share." That sounded good; it emboldened her. "I wouldn't say—"

"Just a minute." Ruth Ann pulled herself up to her full height in the chair. "I understand you're twenty-six years old."

Jennifer nodded.

"Have you ever been married?"

She shook her head.

"And you've never had children."

She shook her head again, even though this last was scarcely phrased as a question.

"Then I wouldn't say you're in a position—"

"Hold on a minute here." Jennifer didn't like the feeling of having walked blithely into a trap. "Just because I haven't been *married*." As if marriage, she wanted to say, were the measure of all experience.

But Ruth Ann had stood up. She was holding the legal pad to her chest like a shield and shaking her head. "I can see this is impossible. Obviously you're here just to pick a fight with everything I say. Clearly you have a tremendous need to justify yourself."

"I don't have any need to justify—" This time Jennifer stopped herself. She was falling into the trap again. Ruth

Ann was defining the terms, and she was playing right into them. "Okay, okay. You've got this speech or whatever prepared." She let her voice get a bit tired on that, so at least Ruth Ann would know how she looked down on the exercise. "Go ahead. Do it."

"Thank you." Ruth Ann's voice was cool.

"Right."

Ruth Ann sat down again, arranged the pad on her lap. She took a few deep, slow breaths, as if she'd been coached to do that when the going got difficult. The light coming in through the window reached just past Ruth Ann's chair, so her new auburn hair had a sheen that was deep and electric, and reminded Jennifer of the woods, a certain dark maple down toward the dairy farm. She wanted to hate Ruth Ann now, to sharpen her mind on that hatred. But instead she felt her mind slackening, floating away from itself, as if Ruth Ann were a movie, a piece of music she was going to listen to; as if, since she could no longer answer or interrupt, she was relieved of some basic responsibility.

Ruth Ann was silently rereading her speech from the top, until she got back to the point where Jennifer had stopped her. "I don't think you can begin to imagine the pain I've had to endure this past month. Because if you could—if you had the least sense of other people outside yourself—you'd have never started playing your games with a man who was a husband and father."

Here Ruth Ann paused for emphasis.

"I was just about your age when I met him. I know what that's like. All you care about is yourself, your own pleasure."

On the word *pleasure* she cast a haughty look up, as if that were something sordid, something she had plainly outgrown.

"But we went beyond that to build something. We

made a home. Had two children. Do you have any idea what that's like—to carry a baby though nine months of pregnancy? To give birth? To know that your body is no longer your own, that it won't ever again be the body he fell in love with?"

Jennifer caught herself shaking her head. No, of course she didn't know those things, but she shouldn't let on that it mattered. It wasn't the *body* he fell out of love with. It wasn't *he* who stopped wanting her, first. Yet clearly their history according to Richard didn't fit into this version. Jennifer looked at Ruth Ann in a wave of confusion and sympathy. Was it possible that Richard had had it all wrong? At the very least, he saw the thing differently. It dawned on Jennifer that maybe the truth of these matters could never be known. Maybe truth was like a body that changed, to fulfill a new function. She pulled herself back from these thoughts; Ruth Ann was still speaking.

"Can you imagine what it's like to have your husband look at you and to feel his *disgust*, after you've borne him two children? And then to find out that for months he's been sneaking off to screw a twenty-six-year-old without a mark on her body."

"Not *screw*." Jennifer knew it hadn't come out loud enough, had come out like a swallow.

"What did you say?"

"I said, 'Not *screw*.' That isn't what we were doing."

"Oh. I see." Ruth Ann rolled her eyes. "Would you prefer *making love*? Would that go along better with your moral sensitivities?"

Now it was Jennifer who took in a deep breath. For a moment there, she'd started to fall in with Ruth Ann, with Ruth Ann's way of seeing things. Yet how could she trust a woman who so plainly dismissed her? "You seem to think—"

"I seem to think that you're interrupting me."

Jennifer gave an assenting wave of the hand. She wasn't supposed to be showing her anger, to let on that anything Ruth Ann said could ruffle her.

"I'll tell you what it felt like. It felt like being used up and thrown away."

Ruth Ann stood, and even though Jennifer couldn't imagine that she was finished yet, she felt she should stand, too. But she didn't move. Ruth Ann had placed her pad down next to the chair, and now she was lifting the hem of her shirt, moving her hands toward the waist of her jeans.

She wasn't serious. She wasn't actually . . . But she was: undoing the button as if in slow motion, moving one hand toward the zipper. What did she think she was going to prove? Jennifer had seen stretch marks; she'd seen the stomachs of plenty of women with kids. But then she remembered what Richard had said at the restaurant. *The muscles down there give out.* How she hadn't wanted him to go any further.

The fly opened out onto a white satin triangle. And then all of it, the jeans and the panties, were down, just far enough to show everything but her pubic hair, her actual cunt. Was it visible on Jennifer's face? Because she wasn't prepared, she could not have prepared for this. Maybe *give out* was the best way of saying it. Whatever held flesh together, whatever made flesh into flesh, had abandoned Ruth Ann's lower abdomen. And to go with that face: haughtier than ever now that she was readjusting the underpants over her secret, closing the zipper; now that she had satisfied herself by disgusting Jennifer, too.

Jennifer pulled up the guard on her face, but it was too late, she had shown something. Ruth Ann sat down and picked up the pad. So this had been a programmed interlude, carefully plotted for its effect. Jennifer wondered what it said on the paper. *Pull pants down. Show stomach.*

Wondered why even that little joke to herself couldn't pierce the shell of the way she was feeling: as if she were implicated now as she had not been before, as if she and not Ruth Ann had sacrificed some vast measure of dignity.

"Maybe you figure I'm doing all this to make you feel sorry. No doubt you think I want him back."

Ruth Ann was speaking again, but it came to Jennifer as though across a great distance.

"But I don't want him. I asked you here today so I could tell you he's yours." Ruth Ann stopped for what seemed a long moment, as if her meaning needed time to sink in. "Take him. I no longer want him."

With these last words, Ruth Ann's expression had shifted from satisfaction to out-and-out triumph, and Jennifer felt herself surfacing from her stupor into a state more like awe. This woman actually believed she was working a transformation here, that *saying* it turned the tables—made her a woman who'd willingly given her husband away, instead of one whose husband walked out on her.

"I loved him." She looked down, reflective, a moment, as if to underline the magnitude of her sacrifice. Then, just as quickly, her chin was up and her eyes were flashing that superior glare. "But there are plenty of things I won't miss. Maybe you haven't noticed the way he leaves dirty razors all over the bathroom. Or the way he sweats up the bed at night."

Jennifer might have laughed if she hadn't been so amazed. So this was the flip side of love, the things one used to console oneself. How could a woman who complained about razors and sweat speak in the same breath of love, imagine she'd ever known how to love him?

Ruth Ann said something about movies Jennifer didn't quite catch—maybe how all Richard wanted to do every night was go out to the movies. When she said he spent half his life on the toilet, Jennifer did have to smile. How many times in the past month had she stood outside the closed bathroom door when a meal was ready, or they were supposed to be on their way out, still too timid to knock or call, wondering what could be keeping him?

"See?" Ruth Ann jumped on the smile, pointed at Jennifer. "You know what I'm saying."

Jennifer blushed, and in the same instant thought of Richard, who liked it so much when she did that. She should not be making herself a party to this degrading display, this intimate, bitter postmortem. She definitely shouldn't be smiling. And yet part of her longed for that sense of womanly conspiracy, or camaraderie, she'd felt in the instant she'd smiled. Two women who loved, or loved and *had* loved, the same man: couldn't they share a few secrets? She struggled to get clear of these thoughts so she could hear what Ruth Ann was saying.

"He may be fine as a lover, but he's a terrible husband. I know you don't believe this now. You're just in the honeymoon stage. Oh, he's great for the honeymoon." She let out a hard, knowing laugh. "Let me give you a piece of advice. Don't ever marry him. With a guy like that, marriage spoils everything. In five years, he'll be leaving you the same way he left me. And if you do anything, don't have a child with him. He's no good at it."

For the first time since Ruth Ann had opened her pants, Jennifer moved her mouth to say something. Whether or not she'd ever marry Richard was her own business, and certainly not a question she'd discuss with Ruth Ann. But this idea that he was no good as a father? This man who slept in the bed with his son, who gave horsey-back rides till he dropped, who seemed to live for the days he saw Benjamin?

Ruth Ann must have realized what she was thinking. She set down the pad and stood up. "Sure, now he looks like a great father to you. Now that he's left his kids and feels guilty." She went to the window and looked out, maybe at the same tree Jennifer noticed, that had already lost most of its leaves. "You missed out on the first four years, when he barely knew his son was alive. When Benjamin was a baby, you know what his idea of playing with that boy was? Sitting on the couch and writing briefs while Benjamin crawled around on the rug at his feet. The big father."

Jennifer didn't know what to say. She'd have liked to come to Richard's defense, but clearly she was out of her area.

Ruth Ann turned back from the window and returned to her chair, though she didn't sit down. She seemed to have recomposed herself. She didn't pick up the pad, but when she spoke it was back in the tone of the remarks she'd been reading. "If this is what it took to make him a better father to his children, then I'm at least grateful for that. I also know you're going to be spending a good deal of time with my kids, and sharing in some of the parenting."

Jennifer nodded, though she'd never thought of her role in exactly those terms.

"I can only hope that in spite of the way you've conducted yourself with my husband"—still that term of possession, even after she'd said she was giving her husband away—"that you're a reasonably sound individual. That being around you will do my children no harm."

Jennifer opened her mouth, but couldn't think of anything to say on her own behalf. She just sat there, hands on her knees, looking as sound as possible.

Ruth Ann sat back down on the chair and crossed her legs. The way she took a deep breath, Jennifer guessed she was coming to her finale, and felt a lifting inside herself. Hadn't Ruth Ann already said the worst things she could say? Wasn't she sounding a more conciliatory note now? Might she not be ready to say she was forgiving Jennifer, just as she was *giving* her Richard, giving the children into her care? She knew in that moment that she'd been right to come, that courage has its rewards, that this forgiveness was what she'd hoped for out of the visit. But then she looked at Ruth Ann's face, its newly icy expression.

"Maybe you imagine that now that we've had this little talk, there are no more bad feelings between us. That we can even be *friendly*." She leaned down on that word as if it were a terrible irony. "If so, I want to assure you that you are mistaken."

Ruth Ann turned a page, and only then did Jennifer notice she was reading from the pad again.

"You were here today, but you'll never set foot in my house again. You are never to call me. When Richard picks the boys up and drops them off, I don't want you to be in the car, because I don't want to have to look at you. Do you understand that?"

Jennifer must have been staring stupidly at Ruth Ann, who stood up in a way that clearly said Jennifer should be standing up also, that her time had run out. Ruth Ann gestured with her hand toward the doorway, and Jennifer circled the room with a glance, as if there were some last secret the walls might impart to her, some final wink of contradictory evidence. From the hallway she stole a look in the wrong direction, away from the door, down into a kitchen that was white and luminous, the way the afternoon sun flooded into it. But Ruth Ann was behind her, urging her on to the door, to the sneakers that waited like reluctant accomplices.

• • •

It wasn't until Jennifer had driven several blocks from Ruth Ann's that she collected herself enough to check the clock in her dashboard. Was it possible? Only one-thirty? She felt she'd been inside Ruth Ann's house for hours, as though the atmosphere of the day and the light should be entirely different. She got to the street where Richard had his office, up on the second story of an old storefront block. She should have turned left but instead signaled right and swung around in the direction that would carry her out toward the river. She'd promised Richard she'd come up to the office as soon as she got done with Ruth Ann. He'd probably been pacing since one, and right about now he'd be starting to wait, to wonder what could be keeping her. The road led her through a few more commercial blocks and then out of town. She stepped on the gas and put the Honda up into fourth. She was accelerating too quickly, but she relished the roar of the engine, as if it came through her foot, down her leg, as if she weren't entirely powerless.

At this season the river was low, with only scattered ripples of movement across a brown surface. From farther up in the hills she caught flashes of flame and vermilion, but down near the riverbanks, the trees held their green, and she could almost imagine that it was still summer, that she could follow the river out and out and not have this tug on her, telling her to turn back. *You won't believe what she did.* She heard herself telling him, heard herself trying to sound brave and smug, to cover the doubt Ruth Ann had planted in her like some insidious virus. *A twenty-six-year-old without a mark on her body.* That was not her. She was more than that, just as Ruth Ann was more than that envelope of liquefied skin. But what about Richard? Who was he?

Coming into Middlefield, she had to slow down. She turned into the gravelly incline of the village boat landing and got out of the car. Richard had promised to take her up here with his canoe—the canoe that still waited in the garage behind the Victorian house. The path down to the edge of the river was lined with goldenrod and Queen Anne's lace, and she thought of the extravagant wild bouquets she'd picked all that summer and placed on her night chest, the mornings Richard was coming. She broke the stalk beneath one broad, perfect white crown, and checked for the single, blood-purple dot that would mark the crown's center. She threw the flower into the water and watched it move off downstream. She tried to tell herself none of it had been Richard's doing, but she couldn't help confounding him with what had gone on at Ruth Ann's. In her mind she put herself back in that living room; she was standing up, facing the woman. *What makes you so sure he'll leave me? That it won't be me leaving him?*

CHAPTER 5

"That's total bullshit."

"Look. You wanted to know what she said. So I'm telling you."

"And I'm telling you what a crock it is." Richard lowered his voice on this, and cast a quick glance back at the door between his office and the reception area, as if it had only just dawned on him that he'd been shouting.

Jennifer lowered herself into the high-backed leather chair opposite Richard's desk, the one that was supposed to make clients feel comfortable. She thought of the road she might have kept driving out on, the river.

"Do you know that for the first year and a half of his life, I had him on my back in one of those kid's packs? Every morning. And I didn't just go for a stroll round the block. Five miles. Every day a different route."

"Listen. I'm not her. You don't have to defend yourself." She wanted to look at him, to convince him of this with her gaze, but she couldn't quite meet his eyes.

"Oh, but obviously I do." He'd started to nearly shout again, but pulled himself up short. He placed his hands down on the middle of the desk and bent toward her. "You think I don't see the way you've been looking at me ever since you walked in here?"

She worked her eyes into a widened innocence. "How?" He stood up straight. "Like you bought it all. Whatever she told you. Hook, line and sinker."

"I didn't *buy* anything." She looked down at her hands, the way they'd twisted up in her lap without her even feeling it. "I'm just confused, okay? Aren't I allowed to be a little confused?"

With that, she heard the break in her voice that hadn't changed since she'd been a child, the break that meant she was going to cry, or going to have to fight not to. She stood up and went to the window. Down on the sidewalk opposite, a woman was pulling a young child along by the hand, a breeze of dried leaves hurrying at their ankles like an airborne current, an undertow.

"You know what else she said?" She turned to face him now, to catch some unwitting flicker of truth in his eyes as she surprised him with this one. "She said you looked at her body with disgust."

"Jesus Christ." He slammed his hand down on the desk. "And you say you're not taking sides?" He sat back down in his chair with a motion more like falling. "Sure, I looked at her with disgust, if that's how she put it. You would have looked at her that way, too. Do you have any idea—" He stalled, and she could see he was trying to frame something delicate, something that wouldn't brand him as the typical, reprehensible male in a fight with two women.

She had to come to his rescue. "Yes."

" 'Yes,' what?" He looked confused, as if he'd forgotten he'd started a question.

"Yes, I have some idea."

Still he wasn't getting it.

"She showed me."

"What?"

"She showed me." She raised her own voice now, only not in anger, not in anger with him. "She showed me her stomach."

Then the tears were actually coming, but he didn't move toward her. He just stared, almost stupidly. When he finally spoke, his voice was nearly a whisper. "That fucking bitch." It was as if Ruth Ann had shown something she'd sworn never to reveal, some skeleton in the Avery closet, a dark piece of evidence that incriminated not her but Richard.

"But if you'd loved her . . ." She tried to catch his eye, hopeful.

"Then what?"

"Then it wouldn't have been so bad, would it? I mean, to look at her. Like if you'd both wanted the second kid and that was just something that happened. Like it happened to *both* of you?"

Richard met her eyes now, but she could see he wasn't exactly following. "But I didn't love her. That's the point, isn't it? I didn't *fall* out of love with her because her stomach disgusted me."

Jennifer almost launched one more *but*, and yet looking at him, the furrows of a new kind of hurt cutting into his forehead, she didn't want to go on with it. "Look, I think we've both had enough of this." She stood up. "I'm going to take off now."

"Sure. That's just great."

"I'm sorry. I just think I need to be by myself for a while. It's been a rough day, okay?"

"Yeah, right. Only for you." He waited to see if that would work some effect, but she did not sit back down. "What are you going to do?"

"Go back to the house. Probably take Jet out." She

started to walk toward the door. "So, you'll be back there, what? Five, five-thirty?"

"You think you'll be ready to see me by then?"

"Don't be stupid."

"Well, you never know these days." He raised his eyebrows and threw up his hands, as if they were discussing some highly unstable phenomenon.

She couldn't help smiling.

He caught the smile and ran with it. "Maybe we can take in a flick tonight. Or just stay home and sweat up the bed." She'd told him about all of that when she'd first come into the office.

They could have probably joked back and forth then, even teased each other into a kiss, but she was already turning the doorknob.

When Jennifer walked into the house, Jet wasn't right there to greet her. That meant one of two things. Either he'd been in a deep sleep, or else he'd done something wrong and was hiding out upstairs in bed, waiting for her to find him and scold him. But before she had time to check in the kitchen for damages, he staggered down, his eyes still half-shut, one ear flattened and one pushed back, inside out, so the pink skin showed and the ear resembled some dark-rimmed jungle flower. He pawed at it, then shook himself until it came right again. "Magnolia." That was a nickname Richard had for him. He liked to tuck both Jet's ears back like that and see how long they would stay.

She'd planned on going out for a walk, but seeing the sleepy dog put her in mind of her bed, the rumpled covers and that salty, shut-in dog smell that Richard complained about, but that she found comforting. She headed straight up the stairs and Jet followed happily. While she was taking her sneakers off, trying not to make the connection between that and Ruth Ann, he settled back into his usual spot. When she was ready, she grabbed his hind legs and swung his rear end off the pillow, down toward the foot of the bed. Then there was room for her. There wasn't much quilt available—most of that was bunched up under Jet—but she didn't need it for warmth, just for atmosphere. She snuggled closer to the dog and touched her lips to the soft fur by his elbow. Richard loved to make fun of the way she got into bed with Jet, how she cuddled him. She played along, even or especially when the joking turned sexual. She draped herself over him in positions of exaggerated embrace, she lathered endearments in her most heartbreaking baritone. *You hunk of dog. You magnificent creature, you.*

"Fuck the dog," Richard would say.

"Fuck *you.*"

"That's what I'm getting at."

Finally he'd clap his hands, boom a long "Out!" and the dog would groan, stretch and hobble off to a less contested location.

It was all very peaceable now, practically ritualized. But when Richard had first started coming that spring, he'd been less patient with the competition. They were standing in front of the bookshelves in Jennifer's study, and though they hadn't touched each other yet, it was plain they were going to, and the look that was passing between them was slow and clear enough it was almost like touch. But then Jet was nosing between them, eyeing Richard sideways as if he scented out his intentions and didn't approve.

"Is there somewhere we can put this dog?" His voice was like a proposition, a caress.

"We can put him out," she said.

For the first weeks of their wild, holed-up May mornings, Jet howled at the window, scratched deep grooves into the wood of the doors, dug trenches and heaps of fresh dirt until Jennifer's lawn blossomed into an embarrassment. But there were long moments when the barking and clawing stopped, or she got lost and stopped hearing them. And what spread in that silence was a different frenzy of sound, of blood and breath: what Ruth Ann had called *screwing*.

Jennifer had once seen a film that used footage from Vietnam: a marine taking a shot and a villager falling, just falling, only over and over, the shot and the fall. The filmmaker had spliced in the same awful moment two, maybe three, dozen times, and Jennifer had always figured the point was to show it until you *had* to look at it, until you *could* look at it, until you became inured. It was in that same kind of jumping, flash, repeat image that she now saw Ruth Ann: the hands on the silver button, the pants dropping. But she couldn't get herself to hold the image of what was beneath them, of that *used-up* flesh; couldn't get herself to say, that could be my flesh, and I wouldn't hate anyone.

Instead she lifted her buttocks from the bed so she could take her own pants off and look at her body. She'd gotten a little broader over the last couple of years, though she was still thin, and she didn't mind the spread of that new curve by her hips, how it gave her a less boyish look; didn't even mind the tracery of white-on-white lines like a scarcely visible web, the tiny surrenders of flesh that made the way for those changes, and marked them. Jet was facing the wall now. He snorted the air, cast a contortionist look back her way and sighed again into slumber. She ran her fingers over the stretch marks—she supposed that was what you'd call them—but they had no texture. It was only her skin, the way she was used to feeling it.

She hadn't masturbated since Richard moved in, but now the desire to get herself free of Ruth Ann, the thought of those mornings that spring, made her want something. On their way down, her fingers paused on the little rounds of her pelvic bones, the taut, white valley between them. Then she licked her index finger and touched herself—lightly, in a tiny circle, the way Richard did sometimes. After she came, she kept making the circles, only slower and slower, until her finger barely was moving. Then she stopped and rested her hand just above the line of her pubic hair. She tried but couldn't imagine what it would feel like, touching that flesh of Ruth Ann's.

"You should have told her that's not how it works. I didn't just make a trade-in on bodies." He hadn't been home for ten minutes, but already they'd landed back in this very same spot. It seemed there was no way for them to talk about what had gone on at Ruth Ann's without being infected by argument.

"I know that. You know that." She could have shouted freely now, but she didn't feel like it. "The thing you don't understand is what it was like trying to talk to her."

"I don't understand?" Richard, however, was yelling, and she had to remind herself it wasn't really at her; it was *through* her, at Ruth Ann. "I had it for eight years, remember?"

"And I suppose for eight years she talked to you with a legal pad?"

"Sometimes."

"You're kidding?"

"No. That was one of her tricks. When she wanted to talk and not listen. She pulled that every now and then on me."

"And how did *you* handle it?"

"I gave her a lot of shit. *Then* I listened. And then at the end I went back at her, point by point."

"You're a lawyer."

"And I wasn't scared of her."

Jennifer wanted to say she wasn't scared of her, either. And really, that wasn't the thing. She could remember a hazy intention as Ruth Ann spoke to mentally tabulate each statement she made, each assertion that needed answering. And she might have given those answers, made a speech of her own, if it hadn't been for Ruth Ann's finale. That's what Jennifer hadn't mentioned back at the office, what she needed to let him know now. The thought of saying it, of repeating aloud what amounted to an order of banishment, started up that insidious little machine of her tears again. But she was determined. "There's something I didn't tell you."

"Oh. Terrific. Another secret weapon out of her arsenal? Maybe she told you I beat her?"

"It's not about you."

He must have seen the look on her face, because he got quiet.

"It's about me. Me and her, really."

"Yeah?"

"She says she never wants to see me or talk to me." She swallowed hard. "She says I can't be in the car when you —" But she couldn't finish. Saying it, hearing her voice quaver over the words like a hurt little girl's voice, she realized both how stupid it sounded and how much it meant to her.

"You can't be in the car when what? When I go get the kids there?"

She nodded.

"Fuck her." He was crossing the living room in long, angry strides, and she was glad he wasn't addressing her tears, wasn't trying to comfort her. "She can't tell you what to do. You can ride in the car whenever you feel like it."

She shook her head. "No, I can't." She took a swipe at her face with her shirtsleeve. "Not after she said that."

"Why the hell not?" He had stopped pacing, and was staring hard at her. "See? You let her intimidate the pants off you. That's just what she wanted."

"No, it's not that. I just don't want to now. See her. Have her see me."

"I don't understand you."

She took a deep breath and steeled herself, the way she used to when she spoke to her father and did not want to cry. "I know it sounds silly, but I wanted everything to be okay with her. Normalized. I wanted a truce." She looked away and breathed again before she went forward. "I wanted it to be like, what had happened had happened, and now we could be—" She stumbled when she got to *friendly,* the word Ruth Ann had twisted as though it were a knife in her. She looked up at him, sheepish, exposed.

"That's not her style."

"Apparently."

He sat down close to her on the couch but not touching. They had scarcely touched since that morning, before she went to Ruth Ann's. "You don't need *her* as a friend."

"I know I don't *need* her."

"Screw it, then."

"I guess so."

"Anything else you're not telling me?"

She pretended to be thinking, remembering, and then shook her head. But there *was* something. She hadn't told him what Ruth Ann had said about never marrying him, never having a child with him. And she wasn't going to tell him. She wasn't going to let Ruth Ann pollute what had to do with just them. "That's about it."

"Then can we forget her and get on with our evening?" In his look, she recognized the hunger from their first days, as if all this talk had made him feel the way he had when he'd been with Ruth Ann, made him feel trapped and then freed again.

"What do you mean by 'evening'?" She gave him a quizzical eye that was anything but innocent. She was thinking about her body in the cream light that afternoon, the slow pleasure he'd taught her.

He took her hands and helped her up from the couch, then drew her close to him. The way their bodies matched up, she could feel him pressing between her pelvic bones. "I mean *this.*"

CHAPTER 6

The day Richard was bringing the baby over, Jennifer took a long walk through the woods, up the mountain. She was surprised at how many leaves had fallen, at the way the hill's curves had begun to emerge through the trees like a thinly camouflaged body. When she got back she started a poem, something she had not done for weeks. She wanted to capture the mountain, that body emerging, and only once she was writing did she discover the panicked nostalgia, the wish to suspend the leaves in their fall. If she'd had long enough, she might have written her way into a name for those feelings, but this time Richard was early. When he walked in the door with only a blue vinyl carry bag, she wondered if something hadn't gone wrong. But David was out in the Volvo, asleep, safely enshrined in his kid's seat.

"So what do we do now?"

"We wait. We check out the window every few minutes."

She checked now, and could just make out the pink

swatch of face inside the hooded suit, that looked to her like a snowsuit, for winter.

Richard came and put his hand on her shoulder. "I can't wait till the little monkey wakes up."

He kept peering out, as if even that scarcely discernible piece of the child were a wonder, right in their very own driveway. He turned to her with the kind of look parents must exchange with each other, all pride and tenderness. She managed a smile for his sake, but it felt tight at the sides of her mouth. Was she supposed to feel some immediate link with this baby she'd scarcely laid eyes on, just because he was Richard's?

"So how long you think he'll keep sleeping?"

"Could be half an hour. Could be just a few minutes. How come?"

"I was working on something."

His face fell, as if he'd expected the two of them to stand and wait, rapt, at the window together. "That Institute stuff?"

With his help, she'd landed a job writing the state Environmental Institute's monthly bulletin. "No. I did that this morning. It's a poem. I started a poem today."

"Oh." His expression turned immediately solicitous, reverent. He respected the fact that she tried to write poetry, so much so that sometimes it made her feel like a fake. "Go on back to it. I'll keep a lookout."

"You sure?" The idea of the poem, as far as she'd gone with it, suddenly seemed insubstantial.

"Of course."

"Well, give a holler when he wakes up."

"Don't worry. You'll hear him."

Back at her desk, she looked at the half-dozen lines on the page, at the many more she'd rejected—not with a single, elegant slash, but with a frantic cross-hatching, dark and dense enough to obliterate any evidence. The falling leaves were there, the mountain as body, coming to light, but as for her fears, they seemed now to have nothing to do with this overwrought landscape. They would more properly find their image in the sleeping bundle outside, the baby Richard hadn't wanted but now plainly adored, the baby she hoped was too young to arrive already against her.

She knew her writing was shot for the day, but she stayed in the study. Her eyes wandered over her postcards and snapshots, and settled on the one of her and Jet, when Jet was a puppy. It was the first winter she'd lived in Vermont, and she'd refused to go back to New York for the holidays. She'd already met Pat, who was taking her under her wing. Pat would arrive unannounced in the late afternoon with eggnog and rum; she'd gotten Jennifer invited to a friend's Christmas potluck. But as Christmas week wore on, Jennifer wished she were home, and realized that home meant New York still, meant her childhood house.

On Christmas Eve she'd seen the girl at the general store with the carton of puppies. The carton was filled with hay, to keep their small bodies warm, and each black-and-white-marbled pup had been collared with a red ribbon. There were seven in all, each of them yelping and leaping clumsily out of the hay, as if they knew they had to compete for affection.

It was the pure black one who caught her eye. He had a clump of hay stuck in his ribbon and wheeled around in a circle to catch it. The hay was still attached when the girl lifted him out of the box, and Jennifer used it to make an extra cushion for him on her car seat. In the picture, he still wore the red ribbon. He fit right in the well of her lap, but his big, telltale front paws stuck out like a warning, or promise. Jennifer also looked curiously younger, though it was only three years since the picture. When she studied herself in the mirror now, she noticed a different quality to her face—a deepening of the eyes, a hollowing out alongside her cheekbones—that she figured was worry, or love.

When she heard the front door slam, she jumped up. She could just picture Richard, sprinting out to the car as though someone's life were in jeopardy. Sure enough, by the time she got to the window, he was leaning into the passenger seat, fumbling and tugging at buckles. She could hear the crying now. Even when Richard lifted the baby out of the seat, it continued: long, inconsolable wails interrupted only to take in air, and then gasps of it. How could such a small creature make so much noise? The door opened like an immediate amplification. Richard rushed him straight to the rug, and then pulled a diaper out of the carry bag. "Here. You change him. I'll heat up a bottle."

As soon as he'd barked his command, he disappeared into the kitchen. It had all happened so quickly she was surprised to look down at her hand and see the white plastic bundle. *You change him.* She considered the baby lying at her feet on the rug, kicking and flailing his arms as if trying to grasp something. His face was so red and distorted from screaming, she couldn't tell what he looked like. She considered the diaper, unfolded it. The inside was a soft, cottony stuff that gave off a clean smell. One end was square; the other had a tab sticking out from each corner. Her eyes traveled from the baby's body, sheathed in the bulky blue suit, to the oddly configured white form that was supposed to bring him a measure of comfort.

"What are you waiting for?"

She turned to see Richard barreling toward her. He grabbed the diaper out of her hand and practically shoved her aside. Then he knelt down to David. With a few quick movements of Richard's hands and a rapid-fire sounding of snaps, the blue suit fell open. The pants underneath it also snapped at the crotch. There were a couple of short, zipping tears and the diaper was off, before she'd even gotten a chance to see how he did it. With one hand he picked up the two feet in their tiny blue sneakers; with the other he slid the new diaper under the shining, puckery bottom. "It's okay. Papa's here now. Papa's changing you." Then he spoke without even looking up at her. "Can you check that bottle? On the stove."

She hurried into the kitchen, where she found the bottle in a pot of barely simmering water. She studied the rubber nipple a moment. "What am I checking for?"

"The milk." He called to her over the screaming. "Is it warm?" When he didn't get an answer, he shouted again. "Shake the bottle up. Pour a little milk out onto your wrist."

The liquid that came squirting out of the nipple wasn't terribly warm, but it wasn't cold, either. She caught the stream with her tongue before it ran down her arm. It tasted sweet, almost chalky.

"Well?"

"I think it's okay."

"So bring it in here already."

Richard had the baby all dressed again, his outer suit off. The old, saturated diaper was lying on the rug next to them. When she approached with the bottle, David wheezed in a breath and held his hands out for it. She could have put it right into those small, reaching fingers, but she gave it to Richard, who passed it along. There was an instantaneous, blissful reprieve: he stopped crying. Now the only sound was a serious, muscular sucking, and the gurgling of formula up toward that pliant brown tip. She stared as if she'd just witnessed a miracle. You didn't stop a baby from crying with love. You stopped him by meeting his needs, by changing and feeding him.

Richard was gazing down at the baby entranced, smoothing back the matted wisps of hair from his forehead. He'd told her David looked like him, the way he'd looked at that age. Now that David had quieted down, she could consider his features. She wouldn't call him a beautiful baby. He did have lovely blue eyes, the color of ice mints, but his cheeks ballooned out like a squirrel's saving his nuts, and his nose was broad and flat, like a duck's bill. She looked at Richard, then back at his son. She had a mean-spirited urge to tell Richard she didn't see the resemblance.

Richard squinted up at her. "Why did you freeze before?"

"Freeze?"

"Yeah. When I asked you to change him."

She looked at the dirty diaper, a margarine yellow beneath the first gauzy white layer.

"Wait a minute. Don't tell me." His eyes widened, as if something genuinely startling had only just dawned on him. "You've never changed a diaper before."

She just glared at him.

"No. I'm serious. You never have?"

" 'You never have?' " She mimicked him, his baffled expression. "Of course I never have. What would I be doing changing a diaper?"

He shrugged. "I guess none of your friends have had babies."

"I guess not."

"Didn't you ever baby-sit?"

"Not for infants."

He shrugged again. "I guess we'll just have to teach you."

The tone of wonderment hadn't left his voice, though the irritation had. He picked up the baby, who was nearing the end of the bottle and sounded like he was sucking in air. "We're going to have to teach her, aren't we?"

The voice he used in speaking to David wasn't quite baby talk, but it was lighter, more lilting, than usual. She liked the sound in spite of herself, but she didn't want to give in to it. Her ears were still stinging from the voice he'd used a minute earlier, the way he'd seemed to forget any love for her in his rush to take care of the baby. Maybe she wouldn't learn to change diapers. Why should she?

Richard had sat down on the couch, and was bouncing David gently up and down, working his leg like a piston. David kept a serious face through the first several bounces, but then he gave in to the smile that was loosening those red, pouting lips. That's when she noticed their mouths, how they were almost identical.

Just then she heard a sound at the window, and looked across to see Jet, peering in accusingly with his furrowed brow. Richard had let him slip out when he went for the baby. The dog must have been scratching at the door, but with all the crying they hadn't heard him. She stood. "I better go let him in."

"Couldn't you keep him outside awhile? Until David gets comfortable?" He stood up, too, and pressed David into his shoulder, as if to keep him from harm.

"He looks pretty comfortable to me."

"Don't you think—"

Jet made a long, grating demand down the door.

"I think the dog needs to come in. Your precious David there may as well start getting used to him."

She didn't wait for an answer, just opened the door. Jet flew in, and it was only once he'd pranced a couple of circles around Richard and David that she noticed: one whole side of him was covered with cow manure. He'd been down to the farm again.

Normally she'd have been cursing the dog, but now she jumped at the escape, the chance for action, that his condition afforded her. She kept a chain screwed into the side of the barn for just this kind of occasion. She led Jet outside by his collar, and hooked him up to the chain. Inside the barn, she found a couple of her old dog towels. Then she turned on the spigot and traced down the hose nozzle. Jet hated the hose. She was sure it was because of the game she'd played when he was a pup, chasing him around the house with her plant mister. She used to laugh as he scrambled for cover after each piddling spray, but now she was sorry. She couldn't scold him for running into the neighbor's barnyard or pastures, maybe upsetting the herd; she had to comfort him, for the trauma of pressurized water. She set the adjustable nozzle head to *light spray*, and got a firm grip on the chain. "Easy does it now." Her voice was a singsong caress. "We've got to clean this trouble dog."

As soon as the water came, Jet jumped back, but she expected that and managed to hold him. He pivoted from side to side under the spray, trying to turn his dirty flank away from her. By the time he was clean, the side of the barn was drenched a dark red and she was soaked from her waist to her sneakers. She rubbed at his fur with one of the towels, which he liked better. She started to shiver from the cold water but prolonged her attentions, dabbing at the hair round his eyes, slicking down his coat with her fingers. As Richard would say when she fawned over Jet too much, he was *only a dog*. But he was hers; she knew just what to do for him, the way Richard knew what to do for his baby.

Back inside the house, she changed into dry sweatpants and socks. Then she went to the kitchen, to check Jet's food and water bowls. Richard had David propped up on the kitchen table, and Jet had already discovered them.

He was sniffing David's pants. The boy put up with that. When Jet started licking his hand, though, David jerked back. Richard scooped him up, and butted Jet in the chest with his knee. Jet squealed and reared back, and it was then that the crying came. She imagined how that tongue must feel on the baby's new skin—rough and strange like sandpaper. But it would only be a surprise. It wouldn't actually hurt him.

Richard was rocking David back and forth, saying, "It's okay. Papa's got you."

Jennifer knelt down by Jet and rubbed the proud expanse of his chest where Richard had kneed him. "He's crying because of what *you* did."

"What did *I* do?"

"You made the dog jump back. That's what scared him."

"Oh, give me a break, will you?"

There it was again: that tone she'd never heard Richard take with her before today. She turned toward the door so he could not see her face. She patted the side of her hip, to signal for Jet to follow her. When she spoke, it was under her breath, from halfway across the living room: "I'll give you a break, all right."

When Richard brought the baby upstairs, she was reading in bed with Jet at her side. At the sound of footsteps, the dog tensed to jump up but she put a hand on his head and whispered for him to stay. Richard's and David's faces popped into the doorway as if it were all a game of hide-and-seek, and they had finally found her. David laughed from the back of his throat, a soft, musical gurgling. Richard spoke up as if he were translating. "May we come in?"

His smile and the dance of his eyes pulled on her like an unspoken apology. Still, she kept her voice cool. "I suppose so."

At the side of the bed, Richard motioned with his head for her to make room. She drew her legs up, and he sat down at her feet, with David secure in his lap. Then he bent toward Jet and ran a hand over his fur. "You can pet the doggie. He's soft."

David looked wary, but he let Richard guide his hand toward the silky down of Jet's throat. Jet lay still for it. When he touched the fur, David let out a stream of baby syllables and turned to her with a look that caught her off guard—like a quick little tug on a place in her chest that she hadn't felt before. His hand reached out for her face and she bent toward him so he could touch it more easily. He patted her hair. Then he brought his fingers down her forehead, over her eyebrow. She closed her eye when he got to her lid. His touch was such a whisper it reminded her of Richard's, the way he explored her face in the dark sometimes, like a blind person learning beauty by feel. The last thing she expected was the jab, the sharp fingernail.

"Ow!"

The hand that rushed to her eye had been supporting David's chest, helping to balance him. Now he toppled toward the dog, who leaped up and gave a startled shake that moved down his whole body into a sharp whip of tail. She didn't see it all very clearly. It was a minute before she let go of her eye, to find her fingers were only wet, and not bloody as she had expected. By then the aggressor was safe in Richard's arms, wailing a loud persecution. She took a tissue from the night chest and dabbed it over her eye that was still watering involuntarily.

Richard hopped around the bedroom with the boy on his shoulder. He did not inquire as to her well-being. But when the screaming had shifted to a moderate wail, he turned to her. "You can't shout at a little baby like that. You can't make those quick movements."

"Quick movements, my ass. That kid practically took my eye out." She checked her tissue to see if she might not find even one pale streak to hold out as proof, as an emblem. Her eyelid and upper cheek still stung with the path his little knife of a nail had made.

"Babies do that."

"Oh. Wonderful."

She stood and went to the mirror that curved up from the top of her flea-market-Victorian dresser. The glass was tinted with age, virtually brown along the sloped edges, and the afternoon light was already fading on this side of the house. Still, she could make out the red punctuation, the welting where the nail had first gotten hold.

"How's it look?" He sounded less concerned than skeptical.

"Oh, I'm sure I'll live, if that's what you mean."

"Let me see it."

She closed her eyes and held her face out to him, but cautiously, ready to wince, pull away. He did not touch her eye. He just put a finger to the place on her cheek where the scratch trailed off. "You'll be okay."

He turned to David, who had twisted around from his shoulder to study her. "It's not good to scratch. You hurt Jennifer. Let's make nice now. Let's show Jennifer you know how to make nice."

Richard stroked her cheek to set an example. *Make nice.* The phrase made her think of her grandmother, her mother's mother, that champion of reconciliation, of baby talk, who kept up a modified version of it even today when she spoke to her grandchildren. She let David go for one stroke, but that's all she was chancing.

Richard put the baby to bed in the guest room at seven-thirty, on a pile of quilts on the floor, ringed by a fortress of pillows. The kitchen table was underneath where he slept, so they whispered through dinner. Richard wasn't in much of a talking mood, anyway. His eyes kept traveling up to the ceiling, the vent. Even when she was telling him something, he seemed to be half-listening for a sound from upstairs. He carried the plates and glasses back to the sink as if one careless touch would shatter them. At nine o'clock he got into bed with a book; he said David was sometimes up for good as early as five or five-thirty.

She sat in the study awhile, shifted some papers, but the silence disturbed her. It wasn't like the silence she had in the daytime, alone in the house; it was precarious, fragile, crisp with imminent sound. The front half of the guest room was over the study. If she tore the sheet with her poem out of the pad, would that wake him? How quietly could she open a file drawer? She had a couple of letters to write, but she rolled her chair noiselessly back from the desk. She would go out for a walk. When she got far enough down the road, she could sing; she could shout out loud if she wanted to.

She wore a down vest, her earmuffs and a pair of wool gloves, and she wasn't sorry. The wind was up and it cut right through her jeans. There was also a moon, maybe three-quarters full, that moved up over a low bank of clouds like a light switching on when she came to the cornfield. The corn had been cut a week earlier, and she remembered the morning she woke to the drone of machinery, then walked out to find the world laid bare and open around her. Now, in the moonlight, the stubble took on a hacked, violent quality, multiplied crazily with its shadows. She did want to yell out but she wasn't sure what to say. She stopped in the middle of the cornfield, far enough from both her own house and the farm down below. She didn't think it out before she shouted, "GO HOME."

Her voice echoed back off the hill, distinct enough she

could hear the two words. She sucked in a cold breath. "GO HOME, DAVID AVERY."

First she made it part of her dream, where it was a storm and wind in the trees, where it was a peculiar new music Richard was making her listen to. Then it woke her. The moon shone right through the window, and she was confused for a moment between night and morning. The crying suddenly shifted one octave up and grew louder. She looked over at Richard. In the light from the window she could see his face clearly. His brow was unfurrowed, and a hint of a smile even played on his lips. She couldn't believe it. Weren't parents supposed to respond? Weren't they supposed to be hooked up to their kids, through some magic of biological circuitry?

"Richard." She pushed against his obstinate weight. "Richard. I mean it. The baby's up."

His body tensed and then he was sitting, propelling himself from the bed. "Help me out, okay? Go heat up a bottle."

The kitchen floor was cold on bare feet. Jet ran circles around her as she got the saucepan and filled it with water. Then she just had to wait. When Ruth Ann had said Jennifer would be taking part in the parenting, she hadn't been sure exactly what that would mean; she certainly hadn't imagined *this*. Having a baby in the house wouldn't be only Richard's concern; it seemed to require her participation. And yet Ruth Ann had handled it on her own, all these nights since Richard had left her. Richard would manage it by himself, too, if he were a divorced, single father. If he didn't have someone like her to heat up the milk for him.

Reluctantly she checked the kitchen clock. It was one forty-five in the morning. The floor creaked above her when Richard started to walk a path between the two bedrooms. The bawling traveled back and forth with him like a rent in the night. It only stopped when she brought up the bottle.

She got back into bed. In a few minutes he slipped in next to her and burrowed under the covers.

"I can't believe you didn't wake up." She said it into his hair that smelled strangely of baby oil, formula.

His only answer was a long, muffled, "Shhh," that she could feel on the skin between breasts. She felt his breath there until she knew he was sleeping. But she couldn't sleep; she was listening. If she trained her ear closely, she could swear she heard David's crying, spinning out from that room in a continuous filament. It was suddenly as if the silence was only a skin on the night, and underneath it, steady as blood, was this sound.

Part
Two

CHAPTER I

Jennifer tried to check the windows of houses as she walked past them. What would somebody think if they saw her? She moved purposefully down the block, as though on her way somewhere, but when she came to the corner, she turned and headed back the other way with equal conviction. She'd gone up and down the same block, what—ten, fifteen times? This time she stopped at the corner and squinted down the forbidden street to where the Honda still sat, tucked in next to the snowbank in front of Ruth Ann's house. She stamped her boots on the sidewalk, but that didn't bring the feeling back, so she started to pace again. This was absolutely the last time she'd come with him. He'd promised he'd just drop the kids off, tell Ruth Ann he couldn't stay. She could still hear the useless sincerity in his voice when he left her off at the corner: "Hang tight. I'll be back in a minute." Of course he'd had every intention of keeping his promise, but when he got there, face-to-face with Ruth Ann—her need to swap notes on the kids, her complaints, her request for *just one small* household favor—even his staunchest resolves seemed to crumble.

The other thing she kept hearing, which made a taunting refrain as she paced, was her own exaggerated good-bye to Benjamin. She'd always marveled that it apparently didn't strike him as odd that she got out of the car two blocks from his mother's house, whatever the weather. He seemed to figure it made perfect sense, that it was just a natural extension of her undefined but clearly inferior status. She'd get out of the car and he'd sit there in the backseat, looking off in another direction, as if nothing were happening. Even Richard was usually too absorbed to give him a cue—too busy missing the kids in advance or trying to second-guess Ruth Ann's mood. Little David always made some noise from his kid's seat; he at least responded to the change in stimuli. But the older boy never so much as looked up.

Finally right around Christmas she'd started doing it: sticking her head back in through the car door and saying a loud, theatrical, "Good-BYE, Benjamin." She never really gave him a chance to answer. She popped her head out and closed the door, strode quickly off to her corner. Maybe the fact that he didn't have time to make good would plant some small prick of guilt in him. Maybe Richard would use the last couple of blocks to give a little lecture on good-byes for Jennifer. Something basic enough for Ben's now-five-year-old mind to grasp, like, "She's a person, too." But so far her strategy hadn't paid off, except in the satisfaction she got from pronouncing that imperious farewell and slamming the door shut to punctuate.

At the end of November, when the weekends with Ben and the baby had started to settle into a routine, she'd spoken to Richard about the good-bye issue. "Oh, that."

He gave a sweep of his hand, half dismissive, half helpless.
"Don't let that bother you."

"But it does." She followed him into the kitchen, kicking a decapitated He-Man out of her path as she went. It
was late in the afternoon Sunday. He'd just come back
from dropping the kids at Ruth Ann's, and was wandering
around the house the way he did at those times, as if he'd
lost something but was mounting only a halfhearted
search. She knew it wasn't the moment to talk to him, to
raise even the remote possibility that his number one son
had a shortcoming. But she couldn't help herself. She'd
been steaming for the past hour, ever since he'd packed
the boys into the car and no one had said a word to her.
"He's no baby. He's perfectly capable of opening his
mouth when he feels like it. He spends two days and
two nights in my house. I don't see why he can't be expected—"

"Let me explain something." He sat down at the table
as if the whole subject exhausted him. "You know what
that kid is? He's a daydreamer. Off in his own little world.
It has nothing to do with you." He picked up the Donald
Duck fork still there from Benjamin's lunch. "You don't
think he does that to me? What do you think it's like when
I drop him off at his mother's house? He sees some kid
down the block and he's gone. Or he disappears upstairs
to his room. Gets lost in his toys up there. It's like all of a
sudden I don't exist."

She would have liked to pursue the point further. He
was a daydreamer, fine. That didn't mean he shouldn't be
taught to extend the basic courtesies. But she could see
that the picture of Benjamin floating away from him, into
the recesses of that other house, was in the way of his
listening.

It probably wouldn't have done much good, anyway.

She hadn't gotten very far with her other talks about courtesy. Why couldn't Benjamin utter a *thank you* when she put a plate of dinner in front of him? Hadn't he ever heard of a question like, "Please, may I have something to drink?" With him, it was simply "I'm thirsty," as if the mere statement of need was enough to require immediate redress. At first Richard made out like she was dead wrong; of course his little boy said "thank you" and "please." So she spent a weekend clearing her throat every time he said, "What's this on my plate?" or, "I'm all out of juice." Then Richard said he'd been thinking about it. He'd realized, looking back, that he and Ruth Ann had never made a big thing about what he called, with a distinctly disdainful twist to his tone, *conventional socialization*. They hadn't needed for Benjamin to be thanking them left and right; they'd just known he appreciated what they were giving him.

"And what about those of us who don't know he appreciates anything?"

But he'd never answered that question. Her desire to hear a child say please and thank you was this narrow, hopelessly middle-class need that shouldn't be foisted onto his children.

For the moment she'd let the point drop, just as she'd set aside most of the things she'd wanted to say about Ben and David in the months since they'd been coming to the house every weekend. Richard spent a lot of time talking about the kids with Ruth Ann—on the phone and at her house, when he went to pick them up and deliver them. He wasn't terribly interested in what Jennifer had to offer. She was convinced that sometimes she could be more objective than he, but what she saw as objectivity in a positive sense, he saw simply as *being outside*. When she tried to make a suggestion, he reminded her that she'd only known the kids a few months, that she had no experience raising children.

However badly he and Ruth Ann had gotten along before, they seemed now to be in perfect accord, at least on the subject of David and Benjamin. Ruth Ann would call a couple of evenings a week when she'd gotten both boys off to sleep. Ben had been having a problem at preschool, kicking and hitting the other boys or flatly refusing to draw. David had said a clear *Mama* for the first time, he'd mastered the motion of throwing a kiss, he'd polished off an entire bowlful of mashed-up banana. Richard dredged up a hundred little incidents from Benjamin's five years of life; he dissected David's most innocuous gestures and syllables. Jennifer didn't like to stay in the room for these conversations, but even from upstairs, she could hear him laughing, and knew that on the other end, Ruth Ann must be laughing, too. It seemed to Jennifer as if the decision they'd made, to keep working at raising the children together, would keep Richard and Ruth Ann always in some measure husband and wife. She couldn't help thinking that as long as she remained an outsider when it came to the kids, she'd be kept outside a big part of Richard.

Mostly she got those pangs when Ruth Ann called. The rest of the week she was just as happy to pretend the children didn't exist. Usually Sunday evening she and Richard went out for a movie and dinner after dropping the kids off, and later that night they'd make love. As a rule they didn't make love with the kids in the house. Richard was afraid the noise would wake them, that Benjamin would walk in; knocking on a closed bedroom door was one more aspect of conventional manners about which Richard and Ruth Ann hadn't seen fit to enlighten him. So Sunday night was Jennifer's time to claim Richard back as her own. In a strange way, it was like an extension of what she'd felt when they were still only carrying on an affair: he was hers only some of the time; she could never completely possess him.

Monday mornings were the second stage of Jennifer's reclamation. When Richard left for his office, she went through the house to collect all the toys and stash them in what was now known as the kids' room. She washed David's bottles and put them away and hid the bags of diapers under the bathroom sink. She restored her house-plants and breakable knickknacks to their usual vulnera-ble perches. Then she began her week in her house as if Friday would never come back, feeling the days spread before her like an oasis.

She'd been anxious to start that reclaiming process today; it hadn't been one of the easier weekends. But now there was no way she'd just set her bad feelings aside. She wasn't wearing her watch—she stripped off even her sim-ple jewelry when David arrived, ever since the day he'd almost pulled the gold hoop right out of her earlobe—but she knew she'd been waiting fifteen, twenty minutes at least. Her toes and her fingers stung, however much she kept moving. She looked down Ruth Ann's street again, to stimulate her own incredulity. She could not blame the woman, though she would have liked to. Richard proba-bly hadn't even told her Jennifer was waiting outside. Ruth Ann probably had *never* known, all the times Jenni-fer had waited and been bolstered by a sense of productive martyrdom, as if the image of her on the street corner in that rain or snow or cold wind was in Ruth Ann's mind, playing softly but irresistibly on her sympathies. She could only blame Richard.

For the umpteenth time she passed the house with the snowman, which had started to melt in last week's brief thaw but was now frozen hard again, so he looked as though he were leaning stoically into the wind. Another yard boasted the start of an igloo, the kind she and her brother used to spend long winter Saturdays building when they were small. She'd tried to get one going with Benjamin a couple of weeks ago but he hadn't been interested, even when she'd built up two layers of snow bricks and made all the bricks for the third. When the baby was taking his afternoon nap, Richard sometimes prevailed on her to take Ben outside to play. His idea of fun was a one-way snowball fight, where he could pelt her as long as he liked and she stood there defenseless.

No doubt about it: the kid was a terrible sport. A few weeks earlier she'd finally refused to play him at checkers ever again. She couldn't stand the charade of letting him win every time, of purposely overlooking the most obvious moves, of putting up a show of surprise when he made the triple jump she'd set up for him, when he miraculously arrived at her side of the board to say, "King me." She'd tried to convert him and Richard to the card game of War, a favorite from her own childhood. There was absolutely no skill involved. Ben had the same chance of winning as she or Richard had, and there was no way to fake it. But every time he lost a war he smashed his cards down and was suddenly stricken with stomach cramps. When he actually ran out of cards, he started bawling and striking out with his fists as if someone had physically beaten him.

This Saturday she and Benjamin had been outside alone, and she'd decided to mount a little lesson in fair play. She let him barrage her with snowballs for a couple of minutes but then she started throwing them back. She packed them loose, tossed them lightly. The first time she hit him, he called out, "Hey!" but she could tell it excited him. He started throwing his harder and faster, and laughed when one of hers exploded against his red ski jacket. She wasn't sure exactly at what point things changed.

Benjamin had a strong arm for his age, and he started adding a grunt of effort into his throws. One caught her on the back of the neck as she bent to the snow, right on that strip of skin between her hat and her turtleneck. She cried out and clutched at her neck, more from the surprise and the cold than because it actually hurt her. He gave a shriek of delight that was starting to have an unhealthy edge to it, and hit her again before she could even stand up. Before he got in his next throw, she ducked down and made the big snowball. She didn't mean to throw it especially hard, or so she would tell herself later, so she would swear to Richard and Benjamin. She stood up with the ball in two hands and looked at him: the broad, smug line of the cheekbones he got from Ruth Ann, the victor's detestable grin. Suddenly he wasn't just a five-year-old boy, but everything that was invading her life. Suddenly part of her wanted to hurt him.

He was dancing on his feet, up and down, side to side, like a boxer. She meant to aim for somewhere near his chest but it was hard, coming down from above him. She never meant to hit him square in the face like that. But now, walking up and down the street in this cold, she was just mad enough to admit that there had been a moment, when the ball was sailing close enough it blocked out most of his head, and then after, before the pieces fell, when the crystals shattered across his face in slow motion—a moment when she wasn't sorry.

Of course she had paid for it after. When the pieces of snow fell, his mouth opened up like a wound and he let out a scream loud enough to bring Richard running. She herself had run up to the boy and tried to take his face in her hands, but he only screamed louder and pushed her away, as if she intended to do him more harm. As Richard came flying out through the door, Ben was shouting, "I hate you."

Richard took the boy up in his arms. "Tell Papa what happened."

Ben was sobbing too hard to speak, and Jennifer figured she'd do well to provide her own version. "We were having a snowball fight. He was dancing around, and one of the snowballs—he got hit in the face."

"You got hit with a snowball?" He spoke into Benjamin's buried face as if he needed to verify.

Benjamin shook his head up and down on Richard's shoulder, then lifted it up. "It was a giant one." He turned to her, the sullen knowledge set in his eyes. He took in a big sniffle, then wiped his nose on his jacket sleeve. "She did it on purpose."

Richard never believed it was anything but an accident, and finally even Benjamin let himself be convinced, let her make him hot cider and cookies. But later, in bed, Richard brought the subject up again. "You can't play so rough with him."

She explained about the ice down her neck, how Ben had started getting wild, started throwing them harder.

"So you started throwing yours harder, too."

"Sure. I figured someone should give him an equal fight for once."

"See. That's your problem."

"What do you mean?"

"I mean, you're responding to him *on his level*. You're acting like he's your equal. He's only a five-year-old. You're supposed to be an adult."

She started to open her mouth but there was no argument. Richard was more right than he even knew. It was one of those moments when she was shamed into a sudden awareness of the difference in their age, their experience. *Richard* was an adult; along with everything else, being a parent had turned him into one. She was only *supposed to be* one, only pretending.

And yet sometimes she tired of this charade of maturity, of having to be an adult and letting the children be children. Sometimes, like right now, on the street corner, she wanted to give in to her most pigheaded, childish impulse, to follow it with the same inspired self-righteousness she'd had when she was nine and ran away on her bicycle. There were two ways that impulse might carry her. She could march down the street and bang on the door at Ruth Ann's house. Or she could head in the other direction. That was it: just start walking, as if she were going to walk home. See how far she'd get before he caught up to her.

She was walking the leg out, away from the corner where she could look down to Ruth Ann's. When she got to the end of the block, she crossed and kept going. She looked back over her shoulder to make sure the car wasn't coming yet. As long as she was doing this, she might as well go for the grand effect. She quickened her pace, fueling herself with the picture of Richard pulling up to that corner and finding her gone. He could stay at Ruth Ann's and talk as long as he liked. She hoped, in fact, he would stay a while longer. A couple of blocks ahead, she could make out the sign for the mom-and-pop grocery that marked the beginning of the commercial center of town. She took her hands out of her pockets and flexed the fingers inside her gloves. She hoped she'd get all the way through the business blocks, that he'd find her somewhere along the three-mile hill that led up to the farmhouse.

Jennifer had gone pretty far that summer she'd taken off on her bicycle. She rode almost five miles, to a park on the opposite end of town. She settled herself on the grass by the duck pond. Before she'd left the garage, she'd filled her bicycle basket with her mother's frozen pecan bars and brownies, and now she opened the first silver foil pack. The brownies were mostly thawed out from the ride in the sun, but still cold enough to be chewy. At home, her favorite way to eat them was right from the freezer, like hard blocks of fudge. Her mother always made out as though she were annoyed when she found the empty foil packs, but she never failed to bake more. Jennifer polished off half a dozen before the stomachache hit her. Still, it wasn't only expediency that drove her to her friend Calley's house. While she'd been eating, she'd realized her strategy was misplotted. What was the sense of spending the whole day in this distant park, where no one would think to look for her? Wasn't the point of running away getting *found*?

By the time she'd crossed town to the base of the hill, she was tiring, but she wouldn't admit the fuse of her anger could be burning down. More likely it was because she never got a full night's sleep when the kids were there. David always woke up at least once—usually two or three times—and she was always the first one to hear him. If she woke Richard, he invariably enlisted her aid, to go down into the freezing kitchen and heat up a bottle. So she'd gotten cagier. When she heard the baby crying, she didn't move. She just waited. She could count on David's first feeble alert growing louder, building inexorably toward its desperate crescendo; count on the fact that finally Richard would wake on his own. When he started to stir, she lay perfectly still. She held her eyes shut as convincingly as she had as a girl, lying in the backseat after the long drive home from her grandmother's; if she didn't blink or crack a smile, she knew her father would carry her. She could feel Richard looking down at her, checking her sleep, and sometimes she groaned and buried her face in the pillow, as if the noise were only driving her deeper. He sighed and cursed, but he did not wake her up then. She heard him carry the crying baby downstairs, where he heated the bottle himself, and after a while the house would go silent. It wasn't as though this stopped her from losing sleep. She usually lay there secretly awake long after Richard came back to bed. But she didn't have to get up and get cold. She didn't have to *do* anything.

When she heard it, there was no need to turn around and look. She knew the sound of the Honda, of Richard gunning it up into third. She was so chilled and punch-drunk from pushing herself up the hill, all she wanted to do was get in that car as quickly as possible. But she moved farther out on the shoulder, kept walking.

Richard stopped the car a few yards in front of her and opened the passenger door. "Don't be an idiot. Get in."

"Tell me about who's the idiot."

He inched the car up another few yards to keep pace with her. "You'll freeze your ass out there."

She stopped. "How considerate of you to notice."

"When I tell you what happened you'll understand."

"I understand I've been out here for—I don't know how long." She peered in at the dashboard to get a look at the clock, but she couldn't see it from that angle. She would have liked to keep up the repartee, but she was really too cold. She got in, but stayed at the far end of the passenger seat and slammed the door hard.

"I'm sorry." He said it without taking his eyes off the road.

She kept her voice haughty. "I'm sorry, too."

"Did you think you'd make it all the way home?"

"I was trying." She took off her gloves. Underneath them her hands were almost purple and chapped-looking. She flipped the heater up to full blast, and rubbed them

110

together. "I thought you were going to tell her you couldn't talk today. Was that really so difficult?"

"Look. I said I was sorry. I shouldn't have kept you outside. But she's having a serious problem."

"This may come as a surprise to you, but I don't give two shits."

She blew on her fingers for emphasis, but she knew it wasn't quite true. The idea of Ruth Ann having a problem did arouse an interest, though not exactly concern. She didn't like to admit it, but she could eke a perverse sense of triumph out of the other woman's bad news. Now that Richard was getting along so well with Ruth Ann, Jennifer alone kept alive the torch of his earlier hatred. She almost had a nostalgia for the days when Richard had felt so much bitterness. Jennifer had absorbed that bitterness from him, and for him, and her own memories of Ruth Ann that summer and fall fanned the flame. Richard had moved beyond all that to the point where he was glad to be part of Ruth Ann's life, where he actually *liked* her. The problem was that for Jennifer, nothing had changed. Ruth Ann was still the woman who'd whispered that she hated his guts, who saw Jennifer as nothing more than unblemished meat, who'd banished her to the freezing street corner.

When he pulled into the driveway, she jumped right out and ran into the house. The first thing she saw was Benjamin's lunch box, on the coffee table where she'd set it out so they wouldn't forget it. Now it would be just one more thing for Ruth Ann to bitch about, one more reason for her to call, to insist that Richard drive back to her house.

He closed the door behind him, and she gave in. "Okay. What is it? What's wrong with her?"

He took off his coat and hat and gloves and hung them

all carefully on their hooks. He came and stood by the wood stove, as if he were the one who'd been out in the cold. Even then he waited a minute before he spoke. "It's her uterus."

"What about it?"

"It's falling."

CHAPTER 2

Jennifer heard the scream from the kitchen. She put down her knife and the stalk of broccoli, but just as she started to turn from the counter she heard Richard's footsteps, heavy and fast down the stairs. "Quick. Tell Papa what happened."

There was no answer except for an amplified wail. She came far enough into the kitchen doorway so she could see Richard, with David up in his arms, and also see Benjamin: standing there with that bewildered look that aspired to innocence, the same look he wore whenever he did something wrong and figured he'd make a shot at getting away with it.

"Benjamin."

The boy widened his eyes, broad and dark brown like his mother's.

"Why is your brother crying?"

"I don't know." Ben tried to hold his eyes up, to keep meeting Richard's, but some stronger force was pulling them down toward his feet. "I guess he fell over."

"You guess he fell over?" Richard rubbed a hand back

and forth across David's bottom. "On the rug? And screaming like that?"

He kissed David, who had quieted down and was now straining around in Richard's arms toward his brother with a look of surprise, a look that didn't yet understand why people hurt other people. If only David could talk, he'd no doubt produce an indictment. Of course Ben had pushed the kid down, just as he'd been pushing him down ever since David had taken his first wobbly, unassisted steps the month before, right around the time of his birthday. Now David could make it most of the way across the area rug before gravity reasserted its claim over his diaper-fat bottom. Make it, that is, if his brother weren't there to prevent him.

"Ben, honey. Look at me."

Benjamin raised his eyes slowly, sheepishly, off the floor. "I didn't push him, Pop."

"You're telling Papa the truth?"

The boy nodded, but the lie was written all over him.

She used to lie a lot when she was a kid, or she used to try to lie. She'd present what she imagined to be her most innocent face, and could never fathom how her parents always saw through it. But seeing Benjamin's I'm-telling-the-truth-Papa look, she almost had to laugh to herself. There was nothing in the world more transparent than little kids' lying, the way it misted their eyes and tugged at their mouths. Richard had to be seeing it, too. He was just too tired to deal with it.

She was tempted to intrude, to propose a moderate punishment—at least a few minutes of "time-out" in his room. She often found herself encouraging Richard to take some kind of disciplinary action with Ben. Part of it was surely his guilt, part of it simply his temperament, but Richard had absolutely no stomach for discipline. And naturally Ben knew it, knew he could do almost anything, and the ax wouldn't fall. She couldn't help thinking it was the same weakness in Richard that made it so hard for him to stand up to Ruth Ann. Jennifer couldn't do a thing where Ruth Ann was concerned, but Ben was here in her house, and he was a five-year-old. Whenever he misbehaved, she could feel it rising up in her, sometimes out of proportion to the actual wrong: this need to gain some control, taking the form of the desire to punish him.

But this time she didn't speak up. She pushed herself back into the kitchen to finish preparing the vegetables. She was making a stir-fry—what she'd figured would be a fast meal—but the rice had almost cooked and she wasn't done chopping yet. She was pretty tired herself. It was Friday evening, but the kids had been there since Wednesday; Ruth Ann had needed the extra two days to go in for some tests. Richard had taken Thursday and Friday off work, and kept Ben out of school. He'd said it could be like a little vacation. But she was writing the February bulletin for the Environmental Institute, with a deadline on Monday. She'd told him if he wanted to take a vacation, that was fine, but she couldn't participate.

Just her luck that Wednesday had been the start of a cold spell—fifteen below zero at night and barely zero during the daytime. She had to admit it was too cold for the kids to do much besides play in the house. And with both the kids there, Richard was always dragging her into it. Benjamin was crying for something to drink, so Richard needed her to change David's diaper. The baby was too restless to be left alone, so wouldn't she please throw together some sandwiches? If she'd had a nine-to-five job, she wouldn't be there to help. But she *was* there, and the *no* that always rose up in her throat stuck like a lump when she looked at Richard—the way, even in the cold house, his face had gone humid, the beseeching arc of his hands. She had her own weaknesses, too: she couldn't turn the other way when he really needed her.

Before she started the stir-fry, she set the table and spooned out David's bowl of evening applesauce. In the living room, Benjamin was calling out for "Hippopotamus Rock."

"Please, no." She said it aloud, almost loud enough that they might just have heard her.

But there was the sound of tape cases clicking together, the snap of a tape going into the deck, and the opening chords of the song she must have heard a dozen times since the kids had showed up on Wednesday. The music was a bouncy, happy, kids' rock 'n' roll that was insidiously catchy, so she'd find that when she was trying to write, the lyrics would go around in her head. *Take a trip on a hip, hippopotamus rock!* She didn't have to look into the living room to picture the scene: Ben was leaping around and falling down on the rug in a spastic version of what he insisted was break dancing. Richard had David up in his arms, swaying from side to side, spinning, dipping him back with a hand to cradle his neck. *Wellll, hippa-hippa-hippa-hippa-potamus rock!* The music unfurled with the counterpoint of Ben's arrhythmic crashes, David's cries of delight. She turned the burner under the wok onto high and watched the film of old oil smoke off. *Take a trip on a hip*—she caught herself, mindlessly singing along in her head, where what had been a dull ache was sharpening.

The tune faded out along its last *hippa*s, and in the silence before the next song Benjamin started: " 'Hippopotamus' again. Come on. Rewind it, Papa."

She heard a few quick steps and the click that stopped the tape. She had to do something. "Enough!"

Benjamin was still whining, and Richard shouted over him. "You say something?"

116

"I said, 'Enough.' I can't handle it."

The room was silent a moment. Then Ben came in with a low, disappointed, "But, Papa." She could just picture his face, that look that managed to combine a demand and a plea, and always worked its magic on Richard.

There was another moment of silence: Papa torn, Papa wrestling with his conscience. Then David came out with a squawk and a "Mama," which he seemed to use not only for *mother* but also for *more*. More milk. More banana. More music.

"The kids really feel like listening."

She poured some oil into the wok and jumped back when it splattered up at her. He couldn't just say, "Yeah, guys, that's enough." He couldn't just go along with her. Instead, he had to put her into this position: Jennifer the ogre, the one who denies. She threw the onions in and started ferociously stirring.

"Jen? How about if I turn it down?"

"Do whatever you want." *Do whatever the kids want.*

When the music came on again, it was lower. She turned the fan on over the stove, and between that and the hissing of vegetables, she could almost block the song out. It wasn't so bad. It was more the principle—to see him just once side against them.

Jet had an uncanny radar for knowing when dinner was over. He always arrived just in time to scour the floor for the least fallen crumb. Dinners with the kids were a windfall. He wasn't too big on vegetables, but he liked rice, and both the boys' chairs and the floor around them were littered with grains. Jennifer frowned on feeding dogs from the table, but she figured whatever dropped was fair game, and thought of Jet as her four-legged cleanup crew. She cleared the table while he took care of the floor. Richard was upstairs running a bath for the kids, who were supposed to be playing quietly in the living room. A quick bath and then David could be put to bed. Half an hour, forty minutes maximum. Then she'd pour herself a glass of wine or maybe even a scotch from the bottle her father had given her. She'd plug in the earphones and listen to some of her own music, probably Coltrane; the bluesy, cathartic saxophone that for some reason made David cry, and that Benny the Break Dancer always dubbed *boring*. She let a slow sigh leak out through her lips and ticked off the kind of interim countdown that helped her segment and accelerate every weekend: She was practically through tonight. Ruth Ann was taking the kids back Sunday at noon. She only had to make it through the next day, and the following morning.

When Jet had done a thorough job by the table and made a run under the lips of the cabinets, he presented himself at the sink. He was ready to be let out, even in this bitter cold; to assume his evening watch in the perfect hollow he'd carved at the highest point of the snowbank alongside the driveway. Thanks to him, she appeared in the doorway in time to witness the incontrovertible evidence.

Benjamin had set up a battleground with his He-Man figures on the living room rug. David had crawled over to watch, and now he picked up Man-at-Arms, who was one of the good guys. He managed to crawl away a few feet with him before Benjamin noticed.

"Hey. That's mine."

But David only crawled faster. He'd almost reached the coffee table when Ben caught up with him. For a second the brothers were locked in an ill-matched tug-of-war. When David let go of the figure, the force of his own doomed pulling recoiled him backward, right into the edge of the table.

She should have gone sooner but now she ran to him, scooped him up the way Richard would. She spread one hand across the back of his head. She was about to start bouncing him, to chant some comforting word in time to his screams, some word that would have just come to her. But Richard was there, hands dripping with bathwater. She swung the baby away. "I've got him." She wanted to tell Richard to go dry his hands, that she had it under control. But here was another tug-of-war: Richard reaching, prying the baby out of her arms, and she was no more a match for him than David had been for his brother.

She could have managed with David, she'd been doing just fine. But however much Richard wanted her to participate in this life with the boys, he liked to imagine that in moments of trouble or pain, no one but Papa would do for his babies. "It's his head," she said, so he'd at least send his comfort to the right spot. "He banged his head on the table." Then she turned to Benjamin, who had quickly assembled his usual innocent look.

When Ben saw her glaring down at him, he went over to Richard and reached up to stroke David's dangling leg, a vision of brotherly love. David's screaming finally stopped, and Richard spared an arm to hug Benjamin in to him. "My two good, tired boys."

Benjamin sprang back from the embrace. "I'm not tired, Pop."

"He isn't exactly *good*, either."

Ben looked at her as if he'd been slapped. Richard stared at her, too, like she'd just said *fuck* or *shit* in front of the children.

"This time I was standing right there. I saw it all. I saw exactly what happened." Her chest swelled, her chin jutted into the air; now she had him. "David didn't just fall and hit his head. His darling brother there pushed him."

119

"I did not." Benjamin's hands had clenched into fists and his stance was defensive, practically martial, like Man-at-Arms.

"Okay. Maybe 'pushed' isn't exactly the word." She bent to the rug and picked up the figure. "He yanked this thing right out of David's hands. That's what made him fall backward."

"Man-at-Arms." Benjamin pronounced the name like it afforded him exclusive possession. "I had him first."

"So you did take him away from your brother?" Richard asked the question as if it were purely informational, and didn't involve any assignation of guilt.

"I had him, Pop. David just came over and took him."

"Haven't we talked about sharing your toys with your brother?"

Benjamin hung his head with convenient contrition.

"Okay." Richard bounced David up to get a better grip on him. "Bathtime. Before that water gets cold."

He was already heading for the stairway when she spoke up. "Richard?"

He turned only his torso, and his eyebrows lifted with an expression that seemed to ask her, *What now?*

"I think something a little more might be called for here."

"Like what?"

"Like some kind of punishment." Her inflection made it almost a question: *Punishment? Have you ever heard of it?*

"Look. It's getting late. That bathwater's sitting there."

She raised her own eyebrows now, to show she wasn't impressed with these mitigating expediencies.

"Benjamin understands he's got to be better at sharing. Don't you, Ben?"

The boy gave a couple of vigorous nods, and didn't look at her.

What he understands is that he can do whatever he likes. What he understands is that he never gets punished. She would have loved to have said it, but she knew that she still would have lost, and refused to lose any more in front of Benjamin. They trooped up the stairs and her eyes followed Richard's back, as hard against her as any stranger's.

She let her gaze drop onto Benjamin's tight little bottom, moving in its perfect immunity underneath the blue corduroy. She'd hated spankings when she was a kid, but she'd also feared and, yes, maybe even respected them. She remembered her father's broad hand, coming down at measured intervals as he counted to five, or ten, or fifteen; she could hear his voice, perfectly calm, as he counted. The few times her mother had ever hit her or Peter, she'd been raging mad, but for her father the spankings had been another matter entirely. Henry Gold was propelled by philosophy, not emotion. When his sense of justice or discipline called for a spanking, he meted it out. She remembered that when she got older— when she was almost too old to be over his knee—she used to notice his expression afterward. She wouldn't have said he looked happy, but certainly satisfied. Now, looking up the stairs toward the closed bathroom door, she tried to imagine what her bottom, or Peter's, had felt like under his regular hand—his hand that always knew, at each given age, exactly how hard it could strike them.

"Give Papa a kiss good night, baby."

With her support, David was standing up on the bath mat, his little penis dangling down between his legs like

some whimsical streamer of flesh. Benjamin was all dry—
he had his pajamas on—but she thought of the way *his*
penis was already starting to look like a miniature version
of Richard's. She'd only seen her mother naked a couple
of times, and she'd been surprised to realize that Marilyn's
small, rounded breasts were shaped so much like her own.

"Give Papa a kiss now."

She let go of David's arms, and he reached unsteadily
out to Richard. He didn't exactly give a real kiss, but he
placed his pouting lips against Richard's puckered ones.
"Ny-ny."

"Good night, sweetheart."

Richard made soundlessly for the door, and motioned
for Ben to follow him. This was the routine. They'd realized a couple of months earlier that things went more
smoothly if she put the baby to bed. When Richard did it,
David wanted to stay up and play; if Richard actually got
him to fall asleep, he woke up and started to cry every
time his father tried to sneak out of the bedroom. With
her, there was none of that; it was pure business. David
didn't get upset at being left alone with her, as long as
Richard slipped out without fanfare, as long as he didn't
make too much of hugging and kissing his darling baby
good-bye. Once she got David into the bedroom, he was
indifferent enough to her presence that he didn't see any
big incentive for staying awake; he certainly didn't cry
when she left him.

Now she quickly patted him dry while he hung on her
neck, and lay him down on the bath mat. She reached for
a diaper and slipped it under him. By the time she turned
back with the bottle of oil, he'd squirmed around so his
bottom was barely over the diaper. She swung him back
by the legs to reposition him. "Make it easy, okay, David?"

With his feet in the air, she ran a stream of oil from his
tiny testicles down the crack of his bottom. That always

made him giggle and squirm some more, but she held fast to his legs; she wanted the extra oil to drip out into the diaper. "Stay." It was the same tone she used with Jet, when she was in a hurry and she had to brush him or rub his belly with flea powder.

When Richard changed David's diaper, he made a whole game of it. He sang a nonsense song he made up as he went. He teased the index finger he called Tom the Tickleworm along the insides of David's pink thighs. He bent all the way down to David's face to rub noses.

She pulled up the diaper's front panel, making sure it wasn't too snug, and secured the tape fasteners. He kicked as she tried to get his legs into the pajamas, but she forced them in.

"Ba."

"I know. You want your bottle. I've got it right here. You'll have it as soon as you let me get you into these pajamas."

When she bent over to do up his snaps, he started to pull on the neck of her sweater. She took hold of his hand and removed it—gently enough, she thought—but he started to cry.

"Okay. Okay." She took the bottle and stuck the nipple into his mouth. "Here's your milk." But he didn't take it up soon enough with his hands and it toppled over onto the floor alongside him.

He started coughing as if someone had choked him, and flailing his arms. She knew in a second he'd be crying outright. The last thing she wanted was Richard running upstairs to rescue him, Richard catching her in one more failure at child care. She grabbed him up from the mat and slung him over her shoulder. She held the bottle until he got a firm grip. A few gentle pats on his back. Gentle pats, gentle words: "Everything's going to be fine. It was all Jennifer's fault. Silly Jennifer."

In the bedroom, they'd set up a single futon on the floor for David's bed, and put up a gate on the door. Richard had bought posters of puppies and race cars and hung them on the wall behind the big bed; across the room stretched an animal alphabet banner. Little by little the room was filling with kids' books and toys, some imported from Ruth Ann's house, some bought new by Richard. He liked to have some surprise waiting for them in the room Fridays, as if every weekend were a birthday or holiday. She turned on the new clown lamp that sat on the night table, and in the dim light, the shapes of the blue plastic slide and the blowup dinosaurs sprung ghostlike out of the shadows. She put David down on the futon and laid the pile of quilts on top of him. Then she went hunting through the rubble of miniature sports cars and aliens for his stuffed wind-up giraffe that played "This Old Man." She turned the key as far as it went. When she sat down at the edge of the futon, David reached for the animal.

His eyes were wide open but she turned her back to him and surveyed the room. What would happen when her parents got the bug to come up for a visit? Since that day in September when she'd told her mother she was seeing a lawyer, she'd let out very little additional information. Yes, she was still going out with him, maybe two or three times a week. No, she wouldn't necessarily say it was *serious*. She didn't tell them that the guy had moved in; she certainly hadn't mentioned he had a wife and two children. Sometimes she asked herself why she was carrying on this charade, but Richard thought it was a good idea, at least for a few more months, until the middle of April, when the state of Vermont would officially declare him a bachelor. In the meantime, her parents were three hundred fifty miles away, and the only time the lie actually affected her was when the telephone rang. Richard could never answer it on the off chance that it might be Henry or Marilyn, who generally managed to call once a week. Usually when Jennifer went to the greatest trouble to rush to the phone—when she had a load of firewood in her arms, or she'd just stepped into the shower—it turned out to be none other than Ruth Ann Avery, with her icy, "Can Richard come to the telephone?"

Jennifer didn't notice "This Old Man" winding down to a stop, but after a moment she realized the air was free of that monotonous tinkling. David's eyes were shut, and he was sucking slowly, to a regular rhythm, but she decided to sit there another few minutes; she wasn't quite ready to bump up against Richard and Benjamin.

Ruth Ann had not called for a couple of days, which was a surprise. She was staying with a friend down in Boston, and had spent the better part of Thursday and Friday at Massachusetts General Hospital. Ruth Ann's condition— the condition she was assuming she had—was known as a prolapsed uterus. What she felt was a pressure, as if her uterus were droping down, as if it were giving in to the tug of gravity. She'd told Richard she could barely stay on her feet long enough to make dinner before she'd start feeling it. She'd find herself getting sharp with the kids and realize it was because of the pain, this feeling of everything being dragged down or dragged out of her. She was sure it had to do with her muscles, the way they'd gone slack; they just weren't holding things in their place like they ought to. Her friend's sister had gotten a tummy tuck after she had her third kid; she'd told Ruth Ann there was a different opeation for the muscles inside, the muscles that held up the uterus, to tighten or truss them up somehow. That's why Ruth Ann had gone down for the tests. She wanted to see if that operation could help her.

The day Richard had found Jennifer storming up the

three-mile hill, he'd seemed so stricken by Ruth Ann's news that Jennifer had almost forgotten her own small ordeal and wound up trying to comfort him. "I know you feel bad. I mean, she was your wife and all that. But it isn't your *fault*. It isn't like something *you did* to her."

He removed her hand from his knee, where she'd been giving him a squeeze that was kind but not at all sexual— a sort of touch she couldn't have imagined with him just a few months before. He stood up from the couch as if he were pushing away from a shore. "You can say that. Rationally I can even think it myself." He looked out the window a long moment before he continued. "I guess I feel like she's paying, and I'm not. We have these two beautiful kids, and now she has to pay for the both of us."

The pain in Richard's eyes was real enough, was his own, and yet she couldn't help hearing Ruth Ann in his words: *You used me up, you threw me away. Now I'm paying for both of us.*

He breathed as if a weight were bearing down on his chest. "How am I not supposed to feel guilty?"

"She *made* you feel guilty, didn't she?"

"She didn't *make* me feel anything."

"Okay. Put it this way." She stood up. She was talking too loudly. The heat of the argument, of making and scoring this point, was suddenly more important than even the way he was feeling. "Exactly what are you guilty about? I mean, would her muscles be any different if you hadn't left her?"

"Of course they wouldn't be."

"So?" She threw her hands up in the air, almost tasting her victory.

But his eyes narrowed and darkened. "You think everything is her against you. Everything gets reduced to your little contest." He took a few steps toward the stove, then spun around to her. "I'll tell you what would be different."

She could feel her eyes stinging, opening wide.

"She wouldn't have to go through this damn thing alone. She wouldn't be so scared. That's what."

CHAPTER 3

With one hand she held Jet back; with the other she shooed father and son wordlessly out the door. The baby had fallen asleep only five minutes before, and she was determined he shouldn't wake up. This was just what she'd hoped for when she'd agreed to Richard's plan. He and Benjamin missed their old Sunday matinees at the movie theater in town; Ben had been complaining that they never got to do anything anymore without David, just he and Richard alone. So Richard had come up with the perfect solution: she stay home with David while they sneak off into town for *Pinocchio*. She could remember seeing *Pinocchio* when she was a girl, remember the sense of dread and remorse that the hapless puppet's adventures instilled in her. Maybe the idea of having your nose grow when you lie would be instructive for Benjamin. Besides, as Richard explained, it would be David's naptime. If they kept him busy all morning, he'd be ready for a good, long one by the time Richard and Benjamin left. With any luck, he'd sleep the whole time they were gone, and she'd have a few hours to herself—a rarity for a Saturday.

She watched from the window until the car backed out of the driveway. She had an additional, unusual reason for wanting them gone. Pat had dropped over one lunchtime that week, with a joint of some homegrown a friend had mailed her from California. Jennifer hadn't been able to smoke it that day; she'd been working on the environmental bulletin. Pat left the joint with her—she said she had a few more back home for herself—and told her to enjoy it when she was ready. "Maybe you should get stoned when the kids come." She didn't say it with the slightest hint of mischief, but rather like a serious prescription. She said her friend Joan, who taught in a day-care center five mornings a week, was high every one of them.

Jennifer must have looked a bit shocked. She liked to get high, every once in a while, but didn't see it mixing too well with work, or with children.

"I don't mean she gets *ripped*." Pat laughed, as if her younger friend had displayed some archaic sexual squeamishness. "Just a little bit buzzed. You know—to take the edge off."

Now Jennifer tiptoed upstairs, and winced at the way Jet barreled up after her. But when she poked her head into the kids' room, David was sleeping, his bottle glued to his lips. She went into her own bedroom and found the joint in her top dresser drawer under a pile of long johns, where she had hidden it. By rights, she should smoke it outside. The cold spell had broken—it was in the low twenties. But she didn't want to consume this uncommon treat like a fugitive. What she wanted was to sit and smoke it in bed. Granted, it was rather close to where the baby was sleeping. But maybe a little smoke wafting in there would be a good thing; maybe it would keep him asleep longer.

As she set herself up in the bed, she thought about what

had happened to Jet when he was a puppy, six or seven months old. Pat was having a barbecue in her backyard, and had made a tray of pot brownies. There were about ten of Pat's friends lying around on the grass, watching the light change color and fade, and feeling the effect of the brownies creep up on them. Jet had been into mischief throughout the affair—chasing a neighbor's Siamese through Pat's prize delphiniums, attempting to heist a chicken breast right off the grill. But now, as the buzz from the brownies got mixed up with the twilight and cricket song, everyone—even Jennifer—let down their guard. No one thought of the platter on the picnic table up by the house, still one-quarter full; no one noticed Jet stealing up on it. It was only when Pat had lit up a circle of citronella candle flares that Jennifer realized the dog was acting different. He cut across the lawn in a series of jerky, lightning trajectories, toppling a wine bottle, crashing into somebody's leg. People started laughing and shouting encouragement, but Jennifer didn't think it was funny. She tried to catch him, only he was moving too fast. Pat came through the back door with a pitcher of tea —the brownies were making everyone thirsty—and called out, "Okay, which one of you drug fiends snitched the rest of these babies?"

"Oh, God." Jennifer instantly knew. "The dog must have gotten them."

She wanted to call the vet up at home; after all, this was an emergency. But Pat convinced her you just don't go phoning a vet and saying your dog ate a quarter tray of pot brownies. They got Jet a bowl of cold water, which he drank right down, and sprinkled some more water on his face for good measure. By the time Jennifer was ready to load him into the car, he'd slowed down. Pat told her not to worry, he'd be like new the next day. Jennifer carried him into the house and set him down on his feet. He walked right into a wall in the living room. He couldn't make it up more than two steps on his own, and his eyes were rolled halfway back in his head. Pat had assured her it wasn't her fault; she hadn't even realized the brownies were sitting there. But still, she couldn't help blaming and berating herself. She was convinced she had failed him, that she'd done his puppy metabolism irreparable harm. Calculated on the basis of weight, what Jet had consumed was the equivalent of her eating almost a full tray of brownies herself, single-handed. He slept about fourteen hours without even twitching. Several times over the course of the night, she got up and checked to see that his heart was still beating. He was wobbly the next morning, but obviously on the mend. Still, it wasn't until a couple of days later, when he was clear-eyed and running sturdily, that she began to forgive herself.

She struck the match and considered the flame for a moment, as if the tiny orange beacon itself were a furtive luxury. The pot was dry enough to light easily, but it was heavy with resin. She held the first ambitious hit as long as she could, but before she could count to six it came coughing out of her. She grabbed a pillow and slapped it over her face. Her lungs burned with each cough but she could feel the buzz spreading, radiating out of her chest and up into her head. When Pat had said homegrown, Jennifer had never imagined something this potent.

She recovered enough to get up and close the door; she could open the room up to air it out after. In the small bedroom, with her joint and her dog stretched out on the rug, she had a comforting sensation of self-sufficiency. She took a fresh hit, this time smaller—small enough she could hold it, until it felt as if the smoke had spread through her body to every limb, every cell. She took another couple of hits like that. She knew it was more than enough but it tasted so good, and she liked the feeling it gave her: that the room was growing round and deepening; that the circle of her body, too, was tightening and deepening, like an aura shrinking but growing denser in hue. By the time she tapped out the burning end with a moistened fingertip, there was less than half the joint left, and the silence in the room, in the house, had acquired a palpable density. For a while she sat listening to her ears open outward, to the sheets of charged air that curled around and sped past them.

She opened her door and creaked carefully into the hall. She didn't bother to step into the other bedroom to check for breathing, a heartbeat, the way Richard always did when the baby was napping. Downstairs, she drank some orange juice out of the carton and then went to the stereo. She flipped through a stack of albums but went back to the first, an old Billie Holiday. She'd played her favorite side enough times it had a permanent static scratchiness that seemed to feed right into the mood of the music. She plugged in her headphones and let the disc spin. First came the opening riffs from the band, and then Billie: *You don't have to have a hanker, to be a broker or a banker. No, sirree, just if thee be my mother's son-in-law.* She turned up the volume before settling in on the couch. Usually, when she was alone, she belted out the words with the record, but now she checked herself. *Ain't got the least desire, to set the world on fire.*

At first she didn't realize it was the telephone. Her eyes were closed, and her head was shaking in time with the band, when the ring broke through. She ripped the headphones off her ears and ran to the turntable, hit *stop.* The phone rang two more times before she got into the kitchen and seized the receiver. "Hello?" She said it in a voice not much louder than a stage whisper, as if there were some chance to preserve David's sleep. But before the answer came back to her, she heard the first coughs accelerating into a wail, like the individuated putt-putt's of an engine about to jump into full, roaring life.

"Jennifer. It's your mother."

The crying practically sounded as if it were coming from the same room. She cupped a hand around the mouthpiece to muffle it.

"You're not still asleep, are you?"

"God, no." She struggled to get her voice natural. "Sleeping at this hour? You think I'm a total degenerate?"

"I don't know. You sounded strange." Her mother paused, as if she were listening. "Is everything all right up there?"

"All right?" David was now punctuating his wordless plaint with screams of *Mama*. "Of course. Everything's fine. How about you guys?"

But Marilyn ignored this attempt to swivel the spotlight. "Are you alone?"

"Alone? Sure. It's just me." And a hysterical baby.

"I thought I heard something."

"Oh. That." She rallied what little cogent mental power she still possessed. "That's the stereo. I'm up in the bedroom, and I've got music playing downstairs." She smiled to herself at this tricky reasoning, recalling the time back in high school she'd gotten high with a friend, and countered her mother's suspicions about the strange smell with a tale of burning hamburgers. But then David let out an unmistakable screech. She tightened her guard on the mouthpiece, but it was too late.

"I could swear I hear someone crying there. You don't have a child with you?"

"What would I be doing with a child over here?" A good question. "It's just this new soul group, Ma. You know.

Sort of gospel stuff. Lots of shouting." As she spoke, she saw a picture of her own transparent lying face at six or seven years old, a picture of Benjamin's.

"Well, all right. Whatever you say." Marilyn clearly wasn't convinced, but there was a useful by-product of her disbelief: she sounded edgy to cut the call short, as if she'd stepped into something she'd rather not know about. "I was just calling to see how you were, that's all."

"I'm fine, Ma. Thanks. I'll call you sometime during the week, okay?"

She hung up and stood breathing hard. David's screams rained down more ferociously; he must have gotten out of bed and pulled himself up at the gate. She wanted the noise to stop but she didn't want to go up and deal with him. She wanted to pretend he just wasn't there. What if she put the headphones back on and turned Billie up louder? She know she was stoned, but she had a moment of what seemed like terrible clarity: If the baby were suddenly to cease to exist, she wouldn't mind in the least. David and Benjamin, too. If both Richard's boys were to disappear from the face of the earth—if she never saw them again—she wouldn't be sorry.

A new sound joined the racket upstairs: David shaking the gate until it shrieked on its hinges, as if he were trying to pull it out of the wall. "Okay." Her shout was as loud and desperate as his cries. "Shut up already. I'm coming."

She stomped fast and hard up the stairs and rushed at him, wrenched the grasping little fingers off the gate. She popped the gate latch out. With one sharp snap of her wrist the wooden diamonds flew collapsing into the side of the door, and she was advancing through the clear doorway. "It's naptime. What are you doing out of your bed?"

In the face of her advance he scrambled back a few feet and then toppled. She swung him up from under her legs and dropped him back onto the futon. His bottle was still half full of milk, and she stuck it into his hands. "There. Let that keep you quiet."

But David waved his arms like some frenzied alert signal, and the bottle flew out of his hand. His screams weren't tiring, just tightening into sharp, efficient outbursts of breath.

"What do you want?" She saw the crazy dilation that must have been fear in his eyes, but she didn't lower her voice; she thought she'd outshout him. "What do you want from me?"

She grabbed him up from the futon, even though he cringed as she came for him. "All right." Now her voice was lower, screwed down tight to a pitch like a threat. She wheeled around toward the doorway, and out to the hall, the bathroom. "I'll change you."

On the tile floor was a bath mat. She set him down on it and reached for a diaper. She pinned one of his wild legs with her knee and held him firm at the shoulders. "You're going to lie still for this."

His free leg kicked at her but she captured it with a hand and forced it down straight on the mat: the willful baby resistance and then the *pop*, the limb buckling. She ripped his pajamas open with one strong tug at the snaps and pulled his legs out of them. One of his heels smashed down on the tiles. That set him to screaming anew, screaming and thrashing both legs about. She got a tight grip on his shoulders and lifted him off the mat. She would set him back down again, firmly enough to make an impression. He looked at her from there in the air and his lips puckered out like a question, the kind of question a child poses again and again. When she brought him down it was hard—harder even than she had intended. So hard she not only heard it but felt it right through her hands: the way his head hit not the mat but bare floor, the impact of skull on ceramic. Maybe it was just that time seemed to freeze, or maybe there really was an instant, before the terrible screaming, when they looked at each other with equal alarm.

I've broken him. That was the first thought she had when her mind moved. *I've smashed him down and I've broken him.* She bent toward his head. The screams leaped up in her face, the fists struck out at her. But that didn't matter. She needed to slip her hand around to the back of his skull. She expected to bring it out warm and sticky, like her own skull had made it, the time when she was a girl and her brother struck her with the metal toy pistol. But it was only the down of his thickening hair, only skin. Only the fine shelf of bone rolling side to side in her palm as he screamed at her.

She slid the other hand under his back and lifted him. She didn't move the one hand from the back of his head. "David. Please." His skull was intact, but what about inside? She got a picture of Richard, and pressed her lips to the baby's slick, burning cheek. *Please, God, make it so he's okay. Make it so I didn't do anything.*

CHAPTER 4

By the time Richard and Benjamin got back from the movie, David was sleeping as if no one had ever disturbed him. She'd made some coffee to bring herself down, but Richard noticed right away that she wasn't herself. She was sitting in the kitchen when he came in—just sitting, without even a book, as though she hadn't been doing anything. What she'd been doing was thinking, and when she looked up at him she could still see this one image of David, like a screen that had fallen in front of her eyes.

"You okay?"

She nodded. She told herself she should jump up, look alive, but it was as if the part of her that could rally were speaking from too great a distance.

"You're sure?"

She nodded again and worked to brighten her expression by raising her eyebrows. She wished he wouldn't look at her so closely, with such sharp concern.

"David slept this whole time?"

She was about to say yes, but she remembered that she'd never gotten his pajamas back on. That would look peculiar, later on, when Richard went up to get him. "He woke up once." She turned away from him, out the window. It was starting to snow—the finest dusting of flakes that she knew would thicken toward evening.

David had cried a long time, but finally he'd gotten quiet enough to let her lay him down in the bed. She'd found his bottle and wiped the nipple clear of dog hair and dust. He took the bottle right up and started to suck. He was still wearing only his diaper that had never been changed; she covered him with his quilt and got an extra blanket from Benjamin's bed. The room was more shadow than light—the curtains were drawn for his nap —but in the dim glow from the hallway she stared at his fingers, his mouth, the easy, trusting relationship they had with the source of his comfort.

His eyes were beginning to close, but when she shifted her weight on the futon they opened onto that unruffled blue, the placid blue of his usual indifference. That indifference settled over the room with his sleep like some kind of grace or reprieve. Was it possible that he'd forgiven her? Or maybe forgiveness was a quality that didn't yet belong to him, the same way he had no notion of blame. Maybe his memory was still like a perpetual clean slate: he forgot as soon as the pain was gone. If that were true, then it wasn't for *him* to forgive her. It was only for her, to forgive herself. For her and her more difficult memory, that kept raising him up in the air, raising him up and slamming him down again.

When she was sure he was sleeping, she crept back to her bedroom and looked into the dresser mirror. She was surprised to see that except for her eyes, the panic still glazing them, she was merely herself. She hadn't visibly changed; her actions hadn't transformed her. Yet she must have been transformed in *his* eyes in those moments when she was shouting and bearing down on him, must have appeared distorted and freakish through the lens of his fear. He, who had seen her like that, would trust her again, was trusting her. But how would she ever trust herself?

Now, in the kitchen, Richard gave up on her and went to look after Benjamin. After a time she heard David stirring upstairs, heard Richard going up to him. When she knew they were down in the living room she came out to check. She leaned her hip into the doorway, as if her interest were merely casual.

Richard looked up at her from the rug where David was on his back with a bottle. "How come he didn't have his pajamas on?"

"Oh. It's a long story." She was less concerned about coming up with an answer than watching the baby, re-asssuring herself he was really all right.

But Richard wasn't dropping the matter so easily. "Sometimes he pushes the covers off." His eyes were disappointed, accusing, as if she'd left his child to freeze in the snow. "He could catch cold, undressed like that."

"Sorry." She hung her head as though she had failed him, and only in this. She walked into the living room, past the rug toward the stairs.

"Why don't you sit down here with us? We can play awhile."

"That's okay." She stopped for a moment to look at the baby: the way his tiny feet curled in while he drank, and his cheeks, dry now, the palest rose-petal pink. She glanced over at Benjamin, who was carefully piling up blocks for a castle. Suddenly he looked terribly small to her, too, the side of his perfect face turned to her like a reproach in the blue winter light. "I don't feel so well."

She went through the rest of the day like that: hiding, not saying much, looking at the faces of the two children across the dinner table as at the shore of a land she was unworthy to enter. When it was time to put David to bed, she asked Richard if he wouldn't take care of it. She told him she had a terrible headache. Again he gave her that questioning look. She was happy to escape to the bedroom, to shut herself in there with Jet. Later, when Richard came in, she could pretend she was sleeping.

She sat in bed for almost an hour before she realized she wasn't hearing any more sounds in the house. She opened the door and looked into the opposite bedroom. The clown lamp was burning on Benjamin's night table. Ben was in his pajamas, asleep, and Richard was sleeping also, with all his clothes on, a book just ready to flutter out of his hand. Usually these days when this happened she woke him, tiptoed in and touched him on the shoulder, the cheek. He would open his eyes and know instantly where he was, why she'd come for him. She'd take his hand and help him from the boy's bed, lead him like a somnambulist back to their own. But tonight she just looked at him from the doorway, looked at Ben and at David. Tonight he could stay.

It wasn't so much the perfect picture they made, the harmony of sleeping breath. It was more that she couldn't face him. He wasn't like the other men she had known, the younger ones, who were just as happy to let a woman drift off into what they construed as her *mystery*; who could fall asleep right next to her and never realize she was shedding a tear. This man made her talk. He wasn't satisfied with "I don't know," with "I just feel like crying." He drove something out of her even when she sincerely believed that she didn't know. How would she ever hope to keep her silence tonight, keep her secret?

The snow had persisted but now was slackening into a lazy whirl of fat flakes that seemed to be not so much falling as floating upward. The moon was up behind the clouds somewhere, setting the whitish sky aglow with an eerie, sourceless light. She bundled up to take Jet out. She'd gotten used to dressing up for the subzero nights, and felt an unaccustomed warmth stepping into this milder evening, as if it were a moment suspended between winter and spring. And yet the snowbanks loomed nearly over her head on either side of the road, closing her and Jet in like a pair of high, chinkless walls. As she walked between them she told herself no one would ever find out. David did not have the words for it. How often she'd been disgusted with Benjamin for taking advantage of the brother who couldn't yet speak. But now, just like him, she would hide behind that silence, rely on it.

She swung Jet around on his leash before they even got to the end of the cornfield. "Sorry, boy." It was the first time she'd spoken, where usually she kept up a running stream of talk to the dog—no more or less nonsensical than some of the chatter Richard made with the baby, except that this talk would *never* be answered.

"Jet, wait." She caught up and crouched to hug him, and found herself crying into the fur on his neck. She gripped his chest tighter and hid her face in his flank. "I'm sorry, boy." She repeated it over and over, even though she knew the apology wasn't for him.

Later, in her room, the tears came again: the same kind of deep, helpless sobbing that used to take her when she was a teenager, and felt her chest wracked so far in she hoped it might shake something loose, something of what made her hate herself. When the bedroom door opened she turned, forgetting in that instant to be ashamed, as if she had no idea who would be standing there.

Richard's eyes blinked against the light. "What the hell's going on in here?"

She took a quick swipe at her eyes with the heel of her hand.

"Why didn't you get me?" He sat down at the edge of

the bed and looked at his answer: her face. He shook his head, as if to get himself fully awake. "I got up thinking I was hearing the baby."

She looked down at her hands and twisted the blanket around them.

He put his hands over hers, touching more blanket than skin. "What happened to you today?" He leaned down to try to look up into her eyes. "Ever since we came home from the movies. Did somebody call?"

She shook her head. Of course, her mother had called, but that wasn't the issue.

"Did anything happen? With the baby or anything?"

She peered up at him. Maybe he was remembering David in bed with only his diaper on; maybe he was feeling his way toward some kind of connection. She shook her head harder.

"Then *what*?"

She bent over and hid her face in her hands.

He put an arm across her back and drew her in to him. "Calm down. You can tell me."

"It's the kids." The words came out strangled, barely audible.

"What about the kids?"

She took her hands off her face, but didn't lift it. "Not them, really. Me."

"Something about you and them? How you're getting along?"

She nodded. She felt like the reticent child in the guessing game: *Where does it hurt? Is it on your knee? On your elbow?*

"Anything in particular?"

She shook her head *no* again. She would tell the larger truth. "It's just everything." She looked down at her lap, hoping he would stop asking questions now so she could think. "It's just me. How I am with them."

"You're not so bad."

She checked his eyes, to see if he actually meant it. "That's bullshit."

He inclined his head to one side, conceding the point. "I'm not saying you couldn't be better."

With that, the tears started to slide again, as though it were he accusing her. She closed her eyes and pressed her fingers into them, as if by hurting them she could shut the other pain out. She felt something flutter in her face: a tissue, his outstretched hand. "I don't know how to."

"Sure you do. You know how to be nice." He stood up from the bed and slipped off his sweater, started unbuttoning his shirt.

She watched the broad wings of his chest as if they were new to her, as if they were part of that other world where she didn't deserve to belong. She wanted to say, *No. Not with them I don't.* When he got into bed, she slid all the way to the wall; she didn't want to be touching him.

"You know what your problem is?"

She shook her head.

"You never have fun with them." He pulled the blanket up toward his chin and moved closer, as though he hadn't noticed she was keeping away. "You want to get them fed and washed and punished and put to bed. But you miss out on all the stuff in between. You never just sit down and relax and play."

"I play with them." Even as she was saying it, she heard the edge in her voice, the defensiveness.

"Sure. When you have to. When it's helping me out. Or filling the space between dinner and bathtime." He was starting to speak loudly but caught himself, and went back to a whisper. "Have you ever once sat down to play with them because you just wanted to? Because it might give you *pleasure?*"

At first she turned half her face to the wall, but in spite

143

of herself she felt his question sinking in, finding the way toward its answer. No, she never had done that, never played with either one of them just for *fun*. She looked at him, her eyes wide. Wasn't that as terrible an admission in its own way as the other one, the one she never intended to make?

He must have taken her look as an answer. "But that's the thing about being with kids. The rest of it is just stuff you have to get done. If you're not having fun, all that's meaningless." His voice softened. "Having fun. Loving them."

"But I don't love them." She said it angrily, as if it were something someone else had done to her. "They don't love me."

"And they never will, I guess."

"What does *that* mean?"

"What it means is you've got to give something to get something back. You've got to put something into it."

She pretended to busy herself with the tissue. She was seeing David's face in that instant, after he'd struck; hearing that sound in her ears, as though it were the back of her own head on the tile, her skull echoing.

"And another thing."

"What?"

"It isn't so different for us."

"Us?"

"Yeah. Me and Ruth Ann. It isn't so different for parents."

"What isn't?"

He put his hand on her leg, as if everything were already fine. "Well, just that we have our bad moments, too. We get tired. We run out of patience."

She moved her leg so his hand slid off. "It's not the same thing."

"Sure it is."

"No, it *isn't*." Her voice had gotten emphatic. She twisted to face him. He could lecture her about being with kids but she knew something, too. She knew how it was even with Jet: how she could lose her temper but there was a brake to it, a natural bottom. "You've got this *reservoir*. This unconditional love."

"That doesn't stop us from getting angry. From needing out sometimes."

"Still."

"Still nothing."

"But you don't know. I mean, the kinds of things I've caught myself thinking."

He didn't flinch. "You think that's any big deal? You think you've thought anything worse than the things I've thought when I got really mad? The things Ruth Ann has thought?"

She shrugged and shook her head as if she were satisfied. There was no use in arguing. Nothing he could say would convince her that he or Ruth Ann had ever honestly wished their kids dead, that he or Ruth Ann had ever willfully hurt them like she had hurt David. Nothing would.

CHAPTER 5

"Papa."

It was just a whisper but it woke her instantly, as if part of her had been on alert. She opened her eyes. There was a cold winter light out the window, the kind of light that comes just before sunup.

The covers rustled; Benjamin was shaking Richard's legs. "Papa."

Richard moaned and rolled over. She sat up, holding the covers tight to her chin. Benjamin, in his orange pajamas, was a small, blurry sunrise at the foot of the bed. "Go on back to sleep. It's too early."

"I'm thirsty." The rasp of his voice did sound dry.

"Get some water out of the bathroom."

"I want juice."

"That's too bad."

"I want to ask Pop." He rustled the covers again.

"Your father is sleeping."

But just then Richard picked his head up. "What's going on?"

"Papa." He sounded triumphant. "I want some juice, Pop."

"What time is it?"

Jennifer had lain down again, with her back turned to Richard. She could see the clock without lifting her head. "Ten past six."

"How about if you wait a few minutes? Climb in and cuddle with Papa."

"Okay." A sudden cold draft slapped her legs. "Here I come." Benjamin had lifted the covers, and was now crawling up along Richard.

"Easy there. Watch those testicles."

"Sorry, Pop." Benjamin slid down into the space between her body and Richard's. They always put the kids to bed with socks on, but Ben must have slipped his off sometime during the night. His foot grazed the top of her thigh, and it was ice cold. She pulled away toward the edge of the bed, held on to her piece of the quilt and yanked it across with her.

"Where'd you get those cold toes?" Richard was rubbing them. "At the cold toe factory?"

"Paah-pa." The covers jumped as Benjamin squirmed. "Stop tickling."

"I'm sorry. That wasn't me. That was Tom the Tickleworm. You want to say good morning to Tom?"

"Okay."

"Ow." Richard's cry was one of genuine pain, but he managed to lilt it up at the end as if he were joking. "Don't hurt Tom like that. You want to tell him you're sorry?"

Benjamin must have taken the tickling finger back in his hands. He proceeded to make a series of loud kissing noises. There was a moment of silence, which was too good to last. When Richard spoke, it was softly again. "Slide up a little more. Tom wants to tell you a secret."

They had a whispered exchange, muted enough she couldn't make out the words. She burrowed deeper under the covers. The bodies shifted on their side of the bed, and a little finger poked into her armpit. She twisted away, but the finger persisted. "Come on." She jerked her elbow back, out of a reflex annoyance, but didn't connect to anything. "Give me a break."

"Papa said I should tickle you."

She didn't answer, just inched even closer to the edge of the bed, as close as she could get without rolling right off. She hadn't slept very well, and the last thing she wanted was to be part of this game, but she was working hard to control herself. More whispering, and then a cold gulp of draft as Benjamin tunneled back out the way he had come. He tiptoed out of the room, and she felt Richard edge toward her back. She moved away from the precipice, until her rear end sank into the soft, humid mass of his groin, and felt it shifting, hardening. He cupped a hand over her breast; his breath was hot on her neck. She opened her thighs just enough so that his penis could move in between them.

But Richard worked his way out of the grip of her thighs. "He's coming back. I told him he could go get some stuffed animals."

"Just what we need."

Sure enough, Ben came striding back through the doorway, his arms heaped with brown and white fur. He walked to her side of the bed, reached across her and dumped the animals between her and Richard. "I'll go get some more."

He disappeared again, and she shut her eyes. She didn't even open them when she heard the crash and the baby cry.

"Papa! David's awake."

"Help him on in here, okay, honey?"

Help him on in here? It wasn't even six-thirty. Hadn't these people ever heard of sleeping-in Sunday? She put the pillow over her head. She didn't need to watch this procession: Ben loaded down with every ratty little stuffed cat and raccoon that had come as rejects from Ruth Ann's house; David racing in on all fours, his face lit up as if crossing the hall were a major pilgrimage, so despicably happy to be starting the day. There was more commotion at the foot of the bed—no doubt Benjamin boosting his brother up, and then climbing up after him.

"Look who's here." Richard's voice had adopted its joyful father-of-a-one-year-old twang. "Are you my little puppy dog?"

David squealed the way he did when Richard swung him up in the air. Ben said, "Let me under, Pop. I want to get warm." She wondered what had happened to Richard's erection, whether it had disappeared as quickly as it had come. What would Ben or David think if they saw it, rising purple and unfamiliar under the sheet? They were often naked together, Richard and the two boys; many nights, he got into the bath with them. She had once come in with clean towels to see David poking at his father's penis, floating shrunken and pink in the bathwater.

"That's Papa's penis." Richard winked up at her. He hadn't taken the baby's fingers away. "Where's *David's* penis?"

David laughed and slapped the water with the flats of his hands.

"Show Papa your own penis."

David just laughed again, so Benjamin reached around him and gave it a tug. Then he looked up at her, with his lips curled as if he were going to say something mean. "Where's *Jennifer's* penis?"

She deposited the towels at the edge of the sink and turned toward the door. "I don't have one."

Now she felt a bouncing shaking the mattress, close to her head. Even under the pillow she was starting to pick up that unmistakable, full-diaper smell.

"Let *me* have a turn."

"Just a second."

"Come on, Papa."

"Up you go. Boom!"

She wasn't sure whose foot it was, but the kick came hard to the base of her spine. "All right." She shot up from the bed like a missile. "That's it."

David shrieked as if the whole thing were calculated for his amusement.

Richard froze with the laughter still in his throat, still choking him. "That's what?"

Benjamin looked at her as if her presence were a surprise, a curiosity.

She crossed her arms over her breasts, her nipples puckered in the chill bedroom air. Trying to be nice was one thing, but this was impossible. "That's the end of it."

After they left she didn't sleep very much, or she didn't sleep deeply. Richard had closed the door behind them but the noise still pursued her, under the door or up through the floorboards. Benjamin stomping across the pine planks like an apprentice elephant. Benjamin shouting, "Papa, where are you?" David wailing, or smashing his toys on the floor. And through it all the refrain of Richard telling them to be quiet, Jennifer's trying to sleep, loud enough it was as bad as any of the sounds *they* were making. Still, she must have dropped off for a time. When she stirred, the clock read twenty past eight and she realized she'd been having the dream again.

There she'd stood on Ruth Ann's front steps, ringing the doorbell, carrying a loaf of her special zucchini bread wrapped in silver foil. She looked around uneasily while she waited, as if she didn't want to be seen there. She didn't really think Ruth Ann was home but she waited for what seemed in the dream like several long minutes, longer than anyone would actually wait. When Ruth Ann finally opened the door, she was pregnant, or in that state of apparent pregnancy in which Jennifer had first seen her. The long hallway was dark, but Jennifer could see a light at the other end, in the kitchen. It was always as if Ruth Ann didn't recognize her at first. When she did, a tired smile spread across her broad face. Her eyes had a kind of clear, limpid sadness, so when she beckoned Jennifer in, it was as if she were an old friend, that Ruth Ann had half expected and half given up on.

This time Ruth Ann had led her past the living room and into the kitchen, which was as empty of the usual signs of life as the living room had been the day Jennifer actually went there. They didn't speak. She sat at the table and watched Ruth Ann moving about the kitchen, making a pot of tea. She moved slowly, as if she were aware at every moment of her thickness, that precarious life inside. She never looked at Jennifer as she worked but that didn't matter. The strongest sensation in the dream was the feeling of relief at being welcomed, just that; the tired warmth Jennifer got from just sitting there.

She twisted away from the clock and put the pillow back over her head. She wished she could fall asleep and wake up again, without the taste of the dream in her mouth. Deep down she knew she'd trade the present hostility for that welcome, that gossamer kitchen light, but she didn't appreciate the reminder.

When Richard came in and sat at the edge of the bed, she kept her head under the pillow. No doubt he needed her to make the kids' breakfast, to get some firewood while they played.

"Wake up, Sleeping Beauty."

"I'm up."

"So when are you going to rise and shine?"

"When I feel like it."

"Listen. I've got an idea." His hand dove under the covers and made for her back.

She pushed it off. "That hand is ice."

"But you're so warm."

"And I want to stay that way."

She pulled the pillow off and folded it under her chin in time to see him smile, as if her bad morning humor were somehow endearing. "Don't you want to know what my idea is?"

She gave him a skeptical, sideways glance. Unless his idea had to do with shipping the kids off, she wasn't interested.

"Here it is. You get up and get moving. We take the guys out for breakfast. Then we have a couple of hours left to head off on an adventure."

"An adventure?" He had to be kidding. "Like what?"

"Oh, I don't know." He draped his arm around her over the quilt. "We could drive somewhere nice. We could go up over the mountain."

"In this weather?"

"Sure. It's a clear day. I bet the view is incredible."

She turned to the window. No arguing there: the panes enclosed four rectangles of sharp winter light. "But what about the roads up there?"

"The roads are fine." He stood up. "So come on." He whipped the quilt off her.

She grabbed it back.

He clapped his hands, as though he were trying to rouse the dog. "Don't be such a sack of bones." He went to the hook on the door and tossed her the terry-cloth bathrobe.

She sat up with the robe in her lap but she didn't go

further. She looked at him: the neat button-down collar sticking out of his baby blue sweater, the optimistic shine in his eyes. *An adventure.* It struck her all of a sudden that he didn't get it, didn't get it at all. He figured their talk the night before would make everything suddenly fine; figured whatever problem she had could be cured by a little good playing.

He went downstairs to give the kids a bite of something to tide them over until they got to the restaurant. She stayed in bed another few minutes, then hoisted herself up. She could have gotten away without a shower but decided to take one. Her soaps and shampoo and conditioner were lined up at the edge of the sink, and the bathtub was full of rubber crocodiles, miniature Disney characters, little toy boats. She tossed them one by one into the milk crate she'd installed by the tub for that purpose, and set her soap dish and bottles down with a resolute plunk. She turned the shower on extra hot and let the water run over her.

In spite of herself she thought of Richard's body that morning in bed. She didn't want the warm little pulse she got from the memory, so she pinched together her labia, hard enough that she felt a sharp current instead. It was the same thing she'd done as a girl, when she'd gotten what she'd later understand were her first clitoral sensations. It was in gym class, in fourth or fifth grade. The girls were climbing thick hemp ropes hung from the gymnasium ceiling, and Jennifer was strong enough to make it all the way to the top. But halfway up this feeling would get her, there between her legs. It didn't make her feel exactly either good or bad; it made her feel helpless. She had to stop climbing and hang suspended over the gym, over the heads of the other girls, who were looking up at her. "Come on." "Don't stop." "You can do it." If she held on with her arms she could twist her legs tight around the rope, press it into her, until she felt only pain, and not those stirrings she didn't know enough to call pleasure.

She took her time in the shower, took her time getting dressed. The last thing she did was put in her contacts. Blinking up from the sink with both lenses in, she got a sudden, sharpened view of her face, the scowl already set into it. Why did she have to accompany them on their little adventure? The same way Benjamin needed a witness to be totally happy at play, Richard seemed to require her presence, her participation, however unwilling or marginal.

She sat down on the toilet lid, leaned her elbows into her knees and rested her chin in her hands. Of course Richard's motives were only the best: he wanted the woman he lived with to get along with his children. And she wanted to please him, wanted to show him she was willing to try. But she wasn't sure she could do it this morning.

Between her feet was the grate for the heating vent. Down below, all she could see was the worn kitchen floorboards, but she could hear Benjamin. "Papa." His voice was screwed up into a whine. "I thought you said we'd be going soon."

Richard's answer came up to her muffled, probably from the downstairs half-bath, where he must have been tending to David. "Just a few minutes, babe."

Next came the sound of silverware banging methodically into a plate. The banging got progressively louder, then left off. "Papa."

No answer.

"Come *on*, Pop." A couple of more bangs, resounding enough she pictured the faded tea rose on her grandmother's heirloom breakfast plate, flying to bits like so many blown petals. "I want to go *now*."

"Would you shut the fuck up."

She didn't mean to say it out loud, to make it more than a private whisper, a hiss. She was surprised at the way the words seemed to jump back at her off the metal grate, its miniature prison. There was a moment of silence, during which she was suddenly aware of how close she was to Benjamin, as if the warm air that puffed up through the vent were his breath. It was like the moment between the time the plate slips out of your hand, and the instant it shatters.

A gasp and a wail, as though someone had smacked him across the mouth.

"What is it, sweetheart? What happened?" Richard's voice bent in a kind of human Doppler effect, until she saw him race past under the grate. She sat back on the toilet seat, so he wouldn't discover her if he looked up.

"She said a bad word to me."

"Who did?"

"She said a bad word and she said to shut up."

"Who? Jennifer? When? She's not even downstairs."

Benjamin sucked in a big sniffle and must have pointed up at the grate.

"Jennifer?"

She held her breath, as if she could stonewall it, hide.

"Hello?"

Still she said nothing, though her saliva was metallic with doom.

"Come in and sit on the couch, okay, big guy? I'm going to go upstairs for a minute."

Richard's steps were quick up the stairs and he catapulted into the bathroom, swinging the door shut behind him. Still, he looked surprised to see her, there where she was. "What did you say to him?"

"I didn't say it to *him*." She stood up, to bolster the dignity of her position. "I said it under my breath."

"What's *it*?" His eyebrows arced together into a single, livid peak. She didn't think she'd ever seen him this angry. She'd definitely never seen him this angry with Benjamin.

" 'Shut the fuck up.' I said, 'Shut the fuck up.' Okay?"

His hands flew up and he slapped them down hard on his thighs. "No. It's not okay."

"Look." She backed away from the toilet, to the front of the sink, to put more distance between them. "He was driving me nuts. It's not the end of the world, is it?"

"It may not be the end of the world. But I see it as pretty serious. I don't think you realize just how serious it *is*."

"Oh? And how serious is that?" She put her hands on her hips.

He paused for a moment, as if to impress her with the gravity of what was to come. "Ruth Ann and I once fired a baby-sitter for telling Ben to shut up. That's leaving aside the rest of the language."

"Then why don't you fire me?"

She got most of the line out before the tears rose in her throat. She pushed past him out of the bathroom. He grabbed her arm but she wrenched it free. She made it into the bedroom and closed the door before he caught up to her. She could feel his weight hitting the door but she leaned into it hard with her shoulder and slipped the latch home. She sucked in a deep breath so he wouldn't hear she was crying.

"Jenny. Open up. I didn't mean it that way."

"The hell you didn't. And don't call me Jenny."

"Listen. This is ridiculous. We've got a little boy down there whose feelings are hurt. Would you open up this door so we can discuss this like two reasonable people?"

She left the door and sat down on the bed. "No."

"Come on."

"No, I said."

She could sense him still standing there, outside the door, but then he turned and walked down the stairs. Part of her was relieved, and yet part of her didn't want him to. She remembered one of her parents' most spectacular fights, when her mother locked herself into the bedroom. "I'm coming in there, Marilyn," her father had boomed. "Even if I have to break that door down." And he did. He heaved into it with his right shoulder, again and again, until the whole doorframe splintered. She could tell from his face that he was feeling no pain. And she liked to imagine her mother, sitting tight on their bed: first her smug sense of inviolability, and then the thrill of those determined blasts, of the wood cracking.

She listened, but she could only hear the most muted shufflings downstairs. In a few minutes, the front door closed, quietly enough he might have still been working at not waking her. The car that started up in the barn was the Honda. That was just like him: to leave the house in the middle of a fight and take *her* car, as if there were no longer such a thing as individual ownership.

Only when they drove off did she unlock the door and step tentatively into the hallway. She listened for Jet, but the house was almost eerily silent. Richard must have let him out earlier, and never gotten him back in. She went to the door and called, bouncing her voice off the hill; her breath billowed white with each elongated syllable. The black shape streaked out from the back of the house, trailing his own cloud of breath. His sides heaved as if he'd run a long distance. He'd probably been down the road, chasing after the Honda, with the kids slapping their hands on the windows, cheering him on. His coat was slick with the cold; she buried her face in it. "Good Jet. What a good boy for coming."

He stood there and let her hug him, let her heap him with praise. She went to the pantry to get him a biscuit, and put him through an elaborate routine of sitting, lying down, sitting back up again, waiting. "O-KAY, boy." Jet grabbed the oversized treat and ran to the oriental rug. The woodstove was burning well, but she threw another log into it. "That'll do it, boy. Okay, coffee time." She was talking aloud to the dog, to herself, the way she did when it was only the two of them. "Now we're going to have a nice, civilized Sunday morning."

She got as far as boiling the water and grinding the beans before it hit her, like a glaring and unforgivable oversight: Ruth Ann. The idea of Benjamin telling her. *She said a bad word and she said shut up to me.* She imagined him, the minute he was released from his car seat at noon, running up the steps to his mother's embrace, starting to cry afresh as if the sight of her had opened the wound again. He told on every little thing his baby brother did. Why wouldn't he tell on her? This was just the sort of thing Ruth Ann would love: positive proof that the twenty-six-year-old slut was endangering her children.

She'd only driven the Volvo a couple of times, and these days even Richard avoided driving it as often as possible. He'd had the battery checked the past week, though. Between the manual choke and a lot of desperate pumping, the engine finally turned. She revved it up to a reasonable semblance of life and then gunned it out of the driveway, even though she knew she should let it sit and warm up awhile. She'd find Richard and the boys at the restaurant and make good; she'd make it up to Benjamin.

The Rainbow Natural Bakery and Cafe: that's where Richard would go, she was sure of it. The plate-glass window was steamed from the inside, and filled with an unseasonable jungle of jade plants and rubber trees. She had every expectation of finding them and so paused at the door, to try to fix on an opening line, a general strategy. A man and woman, probably in their thirties, came bustling up the block—with a Sunday *Times*, without children—and slipped past her into the restaurant. She got a pang of wishing that could be her and Richard: ordering champagne and orange juice; striking a bargain on who'd be first at the Arts and Leisure, the *Book Review*; each one reading out paragraphs for the other's amusement or edification. But it wasn't going to be that kind of Sunday— hadn't been since the start of the weekend arrangement —and she didn't have time for musing. She had to go save herself.

As she'd expected, they were there, at one of the smaller side tables: David up in a high chair, banging a salt shaker down onto the wooden tray table. Benjamin, his face buried in the menu though he didn't yet read, with a scowl that one could interpret kindly as concentration. Richard, buried in the menu, too, looking—alone with his children like that—somehow besieged or beleaguered. She took off her hat and mittens, stuck them into her jacket pockets, and hung the jacket up on the old-fashioned coat tree. She swallowed hard before she began to advance toward the table. She still had no idea what she was going to say, but she had a sudden sense that it was important less for Ruth Ann than for Richard.

Benjamin was the first to notice her. "Look, Papa."

Richard turned, and his eyes did not betray surprise, or anger, or even hurt. He took her in with a clear, steady gaze, almost like Ruth Ann's look in the dream, in her doorway. "So you decided to join us."

"Listen." She turned from him to Benjamin, back. "I'm so glad I found you. Look, about what happened before. I don't know what came over me." She was talking too fast, but she couldn't help herself. She wanted to get it over with. At the same time, she was driven forward by a sense that what she said wasn't true, was only expedient. She knew exactly what had come over her; she still knew.

"Calm down, okay? Pull up a chair." Richard motioned to an empty one at the neighboring table.

She pulled it up between him and Benjamin. The boy considered her warily, the way you might consider a dog who's bitten you once.

"I'm sorry." She bent toward Ben as she said it. She watched his face to see if that might not be enough, but it wasn't. She cleared her throat and looked over at Richard. "I didn't mean it to come out like it did. It was just like something I was saying inside my head. Like something you say if you're mad, or you're crabby."

Ben turned back to his menu. But then he looked up again, his eyes dark and challenging. "My mom gets crabby sometimes. But she never says that bad word."

"I know." She worked at not sounding impatient. "I shouldn't have said it. I'm sorry."

David slammed the salt shaker down from enough of a height that a rain of crystals streamed out of it. Richard leaned over and took the shaker away. Benjamin closed his menu and pushed it aside. "Can we order, Pop?"

"Not until you tell Jennifer you accept her apology."

He whipped his face around as if he'd been betrayed. And she herself was surprised; Richard was actually standing up for her.

"You do wrong things sometimes, don't you?"

"Yeah."

"And Papa forgives you?"

Ben looked from one to the other suspiciously, as if he knew this logic led to a trap, as if his father were in league with the enemy.

"Papa forgives you, doesn't he?"

The most imperceptible and reluctant of nods.

"Well, then, go on. It would be nice if you forgave Jennifer."

His eyes shot quickly up at hers, then down to the table. "All right."

"All right, what?"

"I forgive her."

"Then how about a hug and a kiss?"

She caught Richard's eye and shook her head minutely but frantically *no*. Why did he have to push it this far? Wasn't it more than enough that the boy accept her apology?

But he raised a hand, for her to let him proceed. "Go on."

Ben looked up sheepishly, as if his father had asked him to touch something disgusting, like a slug or a night crawler. He slid down from his chair. She turned her cheek to him, to make it easier. His lips were chapped, with scratchy, hard little crusts, and the kiss was an expulsion of air, a secret act of aggression.

But Richard must have been satisfied with the kiss, satisfied that all was now well with their attempt at a family. Because when Benjamin asked, "Can I get my pancakes now?" Richard gave him a smile that held nothing back.

"You can get whatever you want, sweetheart."

CHAPTER 6

As soon as Jennifer saw her, she snapped her head back down to her omelet. No one else had noticed, but that wouldn't last long. David was gumming a slippery piece of bagel and Benjamin was pushing half a stack of pancakes around on his plate, after he'd insisted he didn't want the kids' portion. She stole another glance toward the coat tree, where a man with a graying mustache and glasses was helping Ruth Ann off with her coat. She wondered if he were a part of Ruth Ann's new social life; if Richard would be hit with a pang of irrational jealousy when he saw them together.

Ruth Ann surveyed the tables, her lips drawn into a confident line, as if she expected to know or at least recognize everyone in the restaurant. When her eye fell on them, she touched the man's arm and said a few words. Then she was on her way over, leading with her hands.

David kicked his feet and grabbed for the prize of her dangling hair. Benjamin jumped up from his seat; if Jennifer hadn't caught it, the chair would have fallen right over. "Mom! How'd you know we'd be here?"

He didn't wait for an answer, just barreled straight for her midsection.

"Easy, now. Remember Mommy said she was sore down there?" She knelt down, placing herself at his level. "Now give Mommy a squeeze. That's my big boy. You don't know how much Mommy missed you." She released him and held him out at arm's length. "Let me look at that face." Her voice was so high-pitched, so saccharine, Jennifer had to wonder if she weren't laying it on a bit thick for the sake of the spectators.

David bashed his hands down on his tray table, to get his fair share of attention. Ruth Ann turned to Richard. "Would you take him out of the chair? It's not a good height for me to be lifting."

"Sure." He stood up, but seemed as if he were making a point of not moving too quickly, not seeming especially at her command. Before he picked David up, he turned to the man, who now stood at the edge of their circle. "How are you?" Richard obviously knew him; the question was more a kind of verbal nod than a genuine inquiry.

The man got out a tight little grimacing smile and put his hands in his pants pockets, as if he were afraid Richard might try to shake one of them. "Good to see you." He couldn't have sounded less sincere; he was probably a friend from around town, from before—one of the ones who'd taken Ruth Ann's side.

His eyes traveled almost as far as Jennifer. She was ready to acknowledge him in his turn, but he pulled his gaze back before it quite reached her.

Richard lifted David out of the high chair and gingerly handed him over to Ruth Ann, who cradled him into her shoulder and rubbed her nose and her lips in the sparse blond spray of his hair. She spun him around in a circle. That voice again: "Yum, yum, yum. I'm going to eat you all up."

The man said he'd get them a table, and retreated to an empty one farther down the same row, by the window.

Benjamin did a little dance in his place. "Can I sit there, too? With you and Stuart, Mom?"

"Sure you can, honey. But Mom has to talk to Papa for a couple of minutes. In private." She mussed up his hair. Up in her arms, David's little fingers were exploring the bodice of her green velour turtleneck, lighting onto her breasts. "If you're done with your breakfast, why don't you go keep Stuart company, and I'll be right over." She didn't seem to notice the plate full of pancakes.

"But I want to be with you."

"I know, darling. Mommy wants to be with you, too. This will just take a minute. And you're coming home to the house today."

"All *right!*" He did a few more frenzied dance movements, all arms and legs, and flounced toward the man at the window table.

Ruth Ann looked across at Jennifer for the first time, as if she were waiting for something. She took stock of the table with a proprietary eye, and Jennifer understood what she expected. She stared down into her mug and took a leisurely draw on her coffee. When she looked back up, Richard's eyes were fixed on her, too. She met them with a look that said, *You better not ask me to move.* She remembered her father telling her the trial attorney's cardinal rule: never ask a question in court that you don't know the answer to. Maybe Richard was also familiar with that dictum, though he practiced a different brand of law. Even she didn't know exactly what she'd come out with, but it wouldn't be to anyone's liking. She had no intention of budging an inch from that table. They could go talk wherever they liked; for all she cared, they could go out and freeze on the street corner.

Finally Richard motioned toward the back of the restaurant, where the cakes and breads for sale were displayed in glass cases. "You want to step over there for a minute?"

"Would you carry the baby?" She didn't hand David up to Richard, but waited for him to lift the baby out of her arms. She shot a look back at Jennifer, at the ring of abandoned plates surrounding her, as if Jennifer hadn't just won a battle—anything but; as if she were somehow to be pitied.

There was a twitch of strain in Ruth Ann's cheek, near her eye, before she turned after Richard. Her steps were tired, and when she reached the counter where he waited, she leaned her weight into it. Suddenly Richard's words came ringing back to Jennifer: *Everything gets reduced to your little contest.* Here was a woman who had trouble standing up on her feet, who'd just gotten back from two days of tests, who might be heading for major surgery. She wanted to jump up, to call the two of them back. To say, *Please. Take a seat.* But it was too late for that.

They were already leaning together, speaking in intimate tones. Ruth Ann did most of the talking. A couple of times, as she spoke, she placed a hand on her abdomen. Richard nodded, or shook his head from side to side slowly, holding onto the baby as if for support. Jennifer craned around to see the man, Stuart, happily conversing with Benjamin. She pushed the plates toward the far side of the table and nursed the last lukewarm sip in her mug. She wished the waitress would come by with a refill, though she didn't need more caffeine; at least it would give her some ostensible purpose for sitting there. But it was as if even in the waitress's eyes she didn't exist, had become invisible.

Finally Richard reached a hand across and touched Ruth Ann's arm—a firm, buck-up-kid sort of grip—and said something to which she nodded three times with her eyes closed. Then they walked back in Jennifer's direction, Ruth Ann coming first. She passed the table without even glancing at Jennifer, her eyes already reaching for the middle distance, the other man with her son. Richard stopped to pick up the high chair. He spoke to her quickly and low, as if she were an embarrassment. "Why don't you take care of the check? She's going to just keep the kids now."

She went back to the register, to make herself known. While the waitress figured the bill, she looked around at their table. Ruth Ann sat with her back to her, in between the two boys, a hand out for each of them. Richard was coercing kisses good-bye. Stuart looked more comfortable, now that he was in his own place and Richard was only visiting, and as soon as Richard left the table, Stuart looked at Ruth Ann in a way that there was no mistaking —as if he hadn't made love to her yet but wanted to; wanted to be more than a friend in the wake of a messy divorce. Jennifer wondered if he knew about Ruth Ann's condition. What it would be like for her to take a new lover: to have him kiss her lips and her breasts and then grope with his hands at her waist while she closed her eyes, so she wouldn't have to see if his face would betray him.

Ruth Ann's brown Saab and Jennifer's Honda were parked almost across the street from each other. Richard transferred the kids' seats and the duffel of clothes. She stood on the sidewalk next to the Honda, but she didn't get in. She'd parked the Volvo just down the block. She didn't know who would drive which, but she assumed they wouldn't be driving together. He slammed the door of the Saab, which was only a year or two old, and had upholstery that looked like real leather. He crossed the street to the Honda. "Hop in."

She waved an arm down the block. "But your car."

"Forget it. We'll pick it up later." He came around to the sidewalk.

"You driving?"

"Sure." He got in and popped the other door open.

She didn't say anything until he'd driven a couple of miles out of town, along the same river road she'd taken the day she'd gone to Ruth Ann's house. The river was snowbound, iced up hard, so it could almost have been a long, snaking, white trench, and she had to work to imagine the water, still moving under it. "I'm sorry for not getting up." This was her day for apologies. "I wasn't thinking about—you know. Her stomach and everything."

"Not her stomach. Her *uterus*."

"Right."

"Anyway, it doesn't much matter."

"What doesn't?"

"Oh, her standing there for an extra few minutes." His words had a fatalistic drone to them, as though he was tired of the subject, yet his hands were gripping tight to the wheel.

"But I thought that's what hurt her. Being on her feet. Having her—uterus—pull down like that."

He took his eyes off the road to glance at her, even though he was heading into a curve. He looked genuinely surprised that she'd be worrying about what might cause Ruth Ann pain. His eyes darted back to the road and he pulled the car toward the centerline. "It's all over."

"What is?"

"Her uterus. Her *reproductive organs*. All that."

"What do you mean?"

He drove for a minute, and she could see his jaw working, though he didn't open his mouth. "She's going to go to some other doctors. She's going to get it checked out. But the guy in Boston told her she needs a hysterectomy."

The word just hung there, as if it had displaced all the air in the car. Her hand rose to cover her mouth and she got a wincing sensation down there, at the opening to her cervix. She pictured the inside of a woman like a cave, a great, dusty emptiness. "When?"

"It depends. This guy could set her up an appointment for sometime in March. But she wants to see some other people first. She wants to read up on it. To *decide*."

"Is there really any alternative?"

He sucked in a long breath, as if he hated to say it. "I don't think so. Not really."

They drove for a while in silence, and she kept her head to her window. He made a couple of turns, but she didn't pay much attention. She could feel the hate she'd been harboring for Ruth Ann fleeing before a new wave of sympathy. She tried to convince herself that a hysterectomy wasn't so terrible. Ruth Ann was thirty-seven years old. She already had her two children. What were those organs anyway but an impractical dowry of flesh, a troublesome vestige? But even more than her mind, her body—something deep in her gut—didn't want to believe it.

She thought of her last visit home, when she'd left Richard alone for Thanksgiving weekend. The morning of Thanksgiving Day, she'd gotten her period. She went straight for her parents' bathroom, to the spot behind the toilet where her mother had always kept a forty-count box of Tampax. But all she found was a toilet brush in its dainty, concealing stand, and the bottle of bleach her father used for soaking his athlete's foot. She ransacked the medicine chests, the cabinet under the sink, the shelves on the inside of the linen closet door. But still it didn't dawn on her.

She presented herself in the kitchen, where her father was reading the paper and her mother was grating orange rind into her cranberry relish. "Hey, Ma, where you hiding the Tampax these days?"

Marilyn kept her eyes down in the mixing bowl for a moment before she looked up, with the expression she always wore when she knew she was going to disappoint her daughter or son. Jennifer's father jumped up from the table, uncharacteristically helpful. "I'll run out and get some. I wanted to pick up a cigar for this afternoon, anyway."

Jennifer retreated to the kitchen doorway, uncharacteristically acquiescent to help. "Okay. Thanks." She looked at the curve of her mother's back, bending again to the bowl. Why should it surprise her that a fifty-three-year-old woman was no longer getting her period? Yet it did. Maybe partly because her mother had never *said* anything. But even more because it seemed to represent a small death. Sure, her mother's childbearing days had been over for decades. But this official and definitive closure still carried a shock with it, still seemed like something to mourn.

And what a quiet and natural passage *that* was, compared to the death that Ruth Ann would be facing.

When Jennifer noticed the road again, Richard was slowing down for the turnoff to Deer Mountain. This was where he had talked about driving the kids. It no longer felt like an adventure but rather a grim, obligatory enactment. There hadn't been a fresh snowfall to speak of for nearly a week, and as he'd predicted the road was well-tended—sanded until only odd patches of white peeked out from the comforting brown, the snowbanks pushed back on both sides to the line of old maples. For a couple of miles the road had only a gentle incline, but then it started to rise more sharply, and out the back window she could see the valley sinking behind them. She kept her head turned that way, and charted the climb by what was left in their wake, the way she had to measure her progress with Richard by what was left broken behind them.

After a while, staring backward got to her stomach, and she turned to face front again. They were almost up to the top, the little turnout with room for a car or two, where every time the view was startling, no matter how often they came: the dizzying drop, the broad valley, and the next spine of mountains that stretched in either direction, as far as the eye could follow it. The first time she'd come here had been with Richard, back in the spring, when the trees were just budding and even clear across to the far line of hills she could see that new halo of color. She remembered thinking as she'd looked out that day how hard it was to imagine actual leaves on the trees, when the buds alone were so beautiful. Her love for Richard had been a little bit like that then, too. It scarcely had a past to look back on, it had no future—only the endless present lovers conspire to imagine in front of them.

Now he came up over the ultimate rise and coasted into the turnout, pulled up the emergency brake. He didn't look out the window, as if he hadn't come for the view. He draped his hands over the steering wheel and lowered his forehead onto them. She stole a quick glance out her side. The snowbank had been plowed close enough to the edge, it looked from the car seat like nothing was holding them back, like one strong gust of wind could blow them right over. She didn't hear him crying at first; it was just his back and his shoulders trembling. She'd seen her father cry like that when her grandmother died—a tight, convulsive crying as if the tears would never come out, would flow inward.

"Richard?" She put a hand on his shoulder. "You want me to just let you cry?"

He shook his head *no*. "Hold me."

She edged to the inside of her seat and reached across the stick shift, the brake, awkward as any teenager in a dubious parking place, reaching for the mysterious body of love. He left the steering wheel and made for her arms. As soon as she held him, she felt the whole of his torso shifting onto her, like a burden shifting, settling. When the sounds started coming, she tried to realign herself under his weight. They *did* have a past and at least a stretch of a future now. But was it really their own? And this pain of his, this weight she was shouldering: didn't it still belong to Ruth Ann more than anyone?

Part Three

CHAPTER I

When they got to the curb by the crosswalk, Ben took her left hand. Richard had taught him to do that, the way she'd trained Jet to sit down at each street corner when they were walking in town; it was that mindless, that automatic, a gesture. *Before you cross, always take somebody's hand. If I'm not there, then take Jennifer's.* On the other side, David perched up in her arm, looking backward over her shoulder, with his new habit of watching things at longer range, squirming to get a better view of what they were leaving behind them. He'd outgrown the blue corduroy Snuggly pack that would have held him secure at Jennifer's chest and kept both her hands free; outgrown it not physically—it was adjustable to quite a large child—but temperamentally. One look at the pack and he pronounced a perfectly articulated, definitive *no*. Trying to force him in was no use; he kicked and waved his arms and screamed, and he was strong enough now it wasn't so easy to overpower him.

As they stepped out onto the crosswalk, Jennifer found herself slipping into a new game. She'd always felt a sense of imposture, being out in public with Richard's children, but now she carried that sense in a different direction: she took on her false role cheerfully, like a convenient disguise. A woman old enough to be the boys' grandmother passed and smiled at them, and Jennifer smiled back, knowing full well what the woman took her for. In that instant, the make-believe almost worked; she could almost imagine what it would feel like, being their mother—the mother of precocious David, with the insatiable, dancing blue eyes, of beautiful, serious Benjamin.

She tightened her grip on each of them, and filled her chest with the air of that counterfeit pride. Then the light turned. She jogged the last stretch of the crosswalk, with David jostling up and down in her arm. A few steps from the curb, Ben pulled his hand free of her fingers and ran for the sidewalk, like a bird taking wing.

David twisted around to watch his brother flying away from them. He waved his arm as if he might actually get the older boy's attention. "Beh!"—that was his name for him; he couldn't yet close the sound on an *n*.

But Ben was already on his way up the block; he wasn't listening. She got a better grip on David, because the way he was leaning she could picture him straining right out of her arms, flying—as if he *could* fly, if only she'd let him —right after his brother. And soon he'd be old enough. Soon David would walk down the street on his own, and the two of them would take the obligatory hand at the corner. For a moment she'd be the young woman with the two fine little boys. And then from either side, as soon as they could, they'd sail away from her.

She was going to call out to Ben herself, but she saw that he'd held up in front of the ice-cream store. It was Saturday, but Richard had some calls to make from his office, so Jennifer was diverting the kids with a trip to get ice cream. Ben already knew what he wanted—a strawberry cone—and she ordered David strawberry, too, in a cup. It was only the last week in March, but they were having a warm spell. The afternoon was mild enough they brought the ice cream out to one of the round metal tables set up on the sidewalk—the closest the town got to an outdoor café. Three chairs described a half-circle around the table, facing out toward the street. Ben took the one not next to but across from her. She had David in her lap, to feed him with a miniature plastic taster spoon. She was squarely back to her usual sense that anyone who saw them would instantly know that she wasn't their mother, that she could be almost anyone else— baby-sitter, neighbor, friend of the family. She'd had that intuition long before she'd actually figured out what it was that gave her away; she'd finally decided it had to do with how she touched, or failed to touch, them. She was holding David now in her lap, she was spooning strawberry ice cream into his mouth. But the holding was not an embrace; the feeding wasn't a game or a tender ritual. This was simply holding, as for necessary support; simply monotonous spooning, in-out, in-out, and probably too fast with something as cold as the ice cream.

Lately, now and then, she'd felt a desire to touch them, when she didn't *need* to—to reach out and put an arm around Ben, or squeeze the pink, dimpled flesh above David's elbow. But these desires came to her as *ideas*, not as spontaneous gestures; there seemed to be an impassable gulf between thinking and doing them. It was like the paralysis she'd sometimes felt with new lovers, when she wanted to touch them or kiss them a certain place, certain way, and yet couldn't bring herself. When she wanted to say something—*I love you; do it softer there*—and the words only grew enormous and taunting inside her.

She pressed a napkin to David's strawberry mouth and followed it when he twisted away from her, but only long enough to get his face presentably clean; she looked at the strawberry running down Benjamin's fingers, and passed him a napkin. They were happy enough with the ice cream, these boys who seemed to her perpetually hungry for anything sweet. Ben was excavating inside the cone with his tongue; David was straining toward the next little spoonful. And yet she knew they should have been happier—happy not just for the ice cream, but to be there with her. What was Richard's word from that winter? *An adventure.* She knew it should be not an errand or sober excursion but an adventure, to go get ice cream with Jennifer.

David lost patience for being fed with the spoon. He leaned down to the table and dipped his fingers into the cup, and she didn't stop him. She was thinking that maybe Richard was right—that things would be different with the kids if she married him.

It had been the past Tuesday, when he'd come home early from work with a bottle of good California champagne and a bouquet of daffodils—the kind of conventionally romantic gesture that wasn't his usual style. He'd gotten the notice that afternoon: his final divorce hearing was set for April eleventh. He and Ruth Ann would appear in court, answer a couple of pro forma questions and sign their agreement. "So listen." He ran a fingertip from her chin down her neck. "I'm going to be an eligible bachelor. Want to marry me?"

She looked from his face to the daffodils and couldn't believe she was hearing right. She'd never particularly focused on the idea of marrying him. She'd always seen his becoming a *single man* as the goal; always figured that once he'd gotten free of Ruth Ann, the last thing on his mind would be binding himself once again in that venerable institution.

He took her surprise as a sign that he needed to work to

convince her. He spread his arms, as if to show off the merchandise. "I'm sweet. I'm good-looking. And, as of April eleventh, I'm *available*. It's not every day you get an opportunity like this."

She made a show of looking him over, to buy herself time. "I suppose you're not *too* bad."

"Well, then?"

She laid the flowers down on the counter and reached for a pitcher. All through these past months, she'd been struggling with the realization that Richard was not truly *hers*. Didn't this mean that he was now ready to more fully belong to her? Wouldn't being his fiancée, and later his wife, give her an edge on Ruth Ann that she didn't seem to have, only being his lover? She would have liked to believe it, would have said yes in a minute if she could be sure. And yet there was something in the sudden, rebound proposal she didn't quite trust, something she could not put her finger on.

Just like champagne and flowers weren't his usual style, being coy wasn't hers. But she'd have to be that way now, until she could find out what he was thinking. "Oh, I don't know." She slipped the daffodils into the pitcher. "I thought I'd experience you as a single man for a while. Don't they say that novelty is the great erotic stimulus?"

He smiled and shrugged, as if it had all been a joke, her clever sally enough of an answer. They drank the champagne and made a nice dinner. They wound up in bed, making love. She was resting her head in the hollow between his shoulder and collarbone when he came back to the subject. "I'm not saying you have to marry me April twelfth. You could experience me as a bachelor for a couple of months, and then we could have a June wedding."

She turned over onto her side and leaned up on her elbow. "You're serious, aren't you?"

"Sure, I'm serious. I'm not in the habit of making facetious marriage proposals."

"Are you in the habit of making sincere ones?"

He sat up. "Are *you* in the habit of being an asshole?"

She sat up herself and moved close enough she was touching him. "Look. I love you, I want you. You know that. I just don't see why you're so anxious to jump back into marriage, after all you've been through."

"It's not just *marriage*. It's marriage to *you*." He brushed off a hair that had fallen onto her arm. "Besides, it would be good for the children."

So here was the catch. "Why for them?"

"Kids like structure. They like things defined. You wouldn't just be 'Jennifer.' You'd be their stepmother." He pronounced the last word with a flourish, as if it were a position of considerable dignity.

She inched away from him and pulled her knees to her chest. So much for the daffodils and champagne, the breathless engagement. "I think being just 'Jennifer' is fine for the moment."

He sighed, as if she were making things unnecessarily difficult. "For the moment. Okay." He slid back down in the bed. "But just think it over."

In the days since, she had thought it over, and every time she did, she realized her thinking had less to do with Richard than with the kids—with Ben, who was now tilting his head to catch the pink drops falling from the hole he'd chewed in the base of his cone; with David, pounding on the table with strawberry fists. The way Richard had put it, it was as if he were asking her to marry *them*. To say she hadn't just fallen into this life with them, but was choosing it.

As soon as she opened the door from the street, Ben squeezed past and ran up the stairs ahead of her. Richard's office was only on the second floor, but the single flight was steep and must have had twenty steps in it. She could feel David's weight in her legs as she climbed, like a stone pulling down on her. By the time she got to the top, she was glad to be greeted by Richard; to pass the child into the arms of his father—the arms that did more than just hold.

"How was the ice cream?"

David laughed, as if ice cream were some silly joke his papa had played on him.

"Hmmm." Richard made a series of smacking noises around David's mouth. "Tastes to me like strawberry. Are you my strawberry boy?"

Ben was hanging on Richard's pants leg. "David had a cup, but I got a cone, Pop."

"A *cone?*" He squatted down, so he was right at Ben's level. "Let's see those hands, then. Okay." He stood up and gave her the eye, as if she could have returned the boys in better condition. "Into the bathroom with both of you."

The office bathroom was around the corner from the reception room. Richard disappeared, with David in his arms and Ben skipping close on his heels. She sank down into the couch, the couch where she'd been sitting the first time she'd seen Ruth Ann, and then Richard, a year and a month or so earlier. She put her head back, shut her eyes and tried to imagine herself as that earlier Jennifer. Her life had been simpler, cleaner, and yet when she tried to put herself back in it, she felt a kind of loneliness she wouldn't have known to feel then. Through the wall behind her came the sounds of the faucet, of Ben and David giggling. The loneliness wasn't only a sense of missing Richard. She had to admit it also had to do with the boys—not *them* so much as an idea they'd started up in her; not anything she actually had with them, but a vision of what she *didn't* have, that their presence kept always in front of her.

Things had gotten better between her and the kids since their low point that winter. No doubt, as time went on, they would get better still, and maybe faster if she turned into their stepmother. Yet wasn't it likely she could only get *so close,* so close and no closer? The love Richard had with them, the love between parent and child: it was something she might approach but would still always stand just outside of. She got a picture from high-school math class—algebra or precalculus—of what, if she remembered correctly, the teacher had called an asymptotic curve: one line approaching another, approaching across infinity but never quite touching. If she wanted what Richard had, if her time with his boys had sown that desire in her, then this curve seemed suddenly to describe her desire, the two-step between her desire and its impossible object.

Richard wanted to take a roundabout, scenic route home, to look at the first signs of the trees budding. She drove. David fell asleep on the first long stretch out the river. She watched him in his seat through the mirror, letting his eyelids droop but then pulling them up again by dint of a visible effort, as if he really wanted to stay awake, to keep seeing. When he was finally out, Richard gestured toward the back for Ben to stay quiet. By the riverbanks, the white birches were deepest in bud; a halo of iridescent spring green seemed almost to float around their thin, supplicant branches. It was after a few minutes of driving in silence, looking at the birches and the light that glinted off the high river as much as at the road, that it came to her. That vision of parental love: she could only *approach* it so long as the child were somebody else's.

But what if *she* had a baby? Wasn't *that* the true shape of this new desire she was feeling?—this desire that now flushed in her like a heat spreading up from deep in her abdomen. A child of her own, that wouldn't fly out of her arms but would cleave to her. She gave a quick glance across the seat at Richard, to make sure he was turned out the window. She was certain something new and disturbing must show in her face. Was the child she wanted, the child she would have someday, *his* child, *theirs*?

She felt herself drifting but caught herself and blinked hard. Here was the road, now curved away from the river; here was the top of the steering wheel. Here was Richard, who *was* looking her way and smiling, who didn't seem to notice anything strange. When he'd asked her to marry him, he'd made no mention of children—except the children he'd already had with Ruth Ann. But wasn't that only because Jennifer herself had never expressed any inclination toward motherhood, because he figured that had to be several years down the road? It couldn't be that the two boys, Ruth Ann's two boys, were all the children he wanted.

She wasn't sure which happened first—whether she woke up or whether, still sleeping, she felt his hands on her. It was all like coming slowly out of a dream, only to find herself inside what she'd been dreaming: the hands, the current that followed his breath down her neck, the way their bodies found each other like swimmers moving up toward the surface. And she found herself thinking, *Maybe I'll marry him. Maybe I'll never make love with another man again.* Because he was inside her, because his arms were circling her from behind and his hands were cupping her breasts, the thought didn't make her sad or even nostalgic. In that moment, she felt that if it were true, she wouldn't be missing anything. She would be swimming up and up, breaking that same surface but never tiring of air.

After the lovemaking, she fell back asleep again. Some time later came the whispering that buzzed around her head for a minute, like a secret she couldn't quite overhear. She didn't stir but felt the bed moving, Richard drawing away. The whispers hovered awhile longer, receded. Still without opening her eyes, without really waking, she shifted toward the center of the bed. A few minutes passed before she heard Benjamin stepping lightly back into the room—heard him or felt him, the way sometimes you sense a presence and turn to find somebody there. She kept her eyes closed as he came closer and brushed the bedcovers. He had a stuffed animal, maybe that new polar bear she herself had picked out for him. That's what it felt like when he placed it down next to her, so the fur was just grazing her cheek. He tiptoed away from the bed and she opened her eyes, but all she could see was the white of the bear, the lazy curve of its belly.

When she heard him coming back, she quickly shut her eyes again. This time the animal's fur was older, more worn feeling, against the back of her neck, and though it didn't touch her she could tell he set another one over her head, on the upper edge of her pillow. She would pretend to keep sleeping all the while he traveled back and forth and surrounded her. Then she'd open her eyes and smile at him as if she were just waking up, as if he'd surprised her, and the animals would be a cushioning halo, a bouquet he had picked for her.

There were many animals, many trips in and out. After a time, all of the movements confused her, until she imagined that she was already his stepmother, that the boy loved her. As she was lying there, pretending to sleep, it was also as if she stood apart, watching—seeing the little boy with the elephant and the leopard, seeing the woman encircled: her eyelids fluttering ever so slightly, that wisp of a smile on her lips. It was because she was also standing apart that she saw him place the last animal and take a step backward, to admire what he'd made; that she knew it was time to quit her pretending.

She opened her eyes. But what she saw wasn't the garden of fur, the little face waiting. She blinked, looked again. She had fooled herself. It was only the bed. Only her alone in a bedroom suddenly larger and empty with light.

CHAPTER 2

There they were, poking out of one of the last, stubborn patches of snow, right where Jet had made his nest all that winter. It wasn't much; it certainly wasn't *flowers*—just the slender shoots of leaves, with the white striping out through the green like a reminder of winter. But for Jennifer, the leaves alone were enough of a miracle. She'd never had the touch of someone like Pat, who seemed to make everything grow, who was always cheerfully complaining about flower beds choking with blooms, about all the work it took to keep dividing and thinning them. Jennifer had a couple of houseplants that had hung on for years—the kind that could tolerate lengthy droughts of neglect. The others came and went, with the seasons of her good intentions. Still, she'd had her heart set on planting these crocuses. She remembered her last-ditch rally to get in the bulbs, just before she went home for Thanksgiving. The ground had already started to harden and it hurt her fingers to break up the clods of cold dirt. An icy drizzle was falling, but she wasn't going into the house until those twenty promises were safely into the soil, according to at least a rough approximation of the feed store's instructions. Now she turned her face to the sun and felt a childish glee, as if she'd pulled something over on somebody.

"Jennifer." It was Benjamin at the front door.

"Over here. Don't let the dog through." Jet would surely trample the crocuses.

"Can I come out?"

"Don't you think you should put on a jacket?"

He disappeared back through the door, but didn't close it entirely. She was about to go shut it herself when he reemerged with the royal blue, satin-finish baseball jacket Richard had bought him the previous weekend. She wanted to send him back to put on his old parka, but what was the point of trying to keep this one new? He walked down the path with an extra jaunt in his step. "Look what I've got."

"I noticed." He *was* cute in the jacket. "Looks good." She checked again for the crocus leaves, as if to make sure. "Come here. I've got something to show you." She motioned him to circle around behind her. "Crocuses."

"Where?"

She bent down and pointed to the leaves showing out of the snow.

"Oh. Those." He did not sound impressed. "We have a bunch of *flowers* already at Mom's house. Yellow and purple ones."

"That's nice." She kept her voice cheery. "I guess it's warmer down there in town than here on the mountain."

But he wasn't listening to her explanation of why his mother's crocuses weren't *innately* superior. He'd walked past the patch that had been the snowbank and was looking up into the tree just beyond it, a silver poplar, with a dense wheel of branches jutting out like spokes from the trunk. "Can I climb it?"

She looked at the size of the boy and the size of the space between limbs, at the shiny new jacket. "Have you ever climbed trees before?"

"Are you crazy?" This was his latest expression, one of the gems imported from preschool. She found it a bit disrespectful, but Richard had decided they could let it go by. "There's a tree at school we climb all the time. Much bigger than this." He raised both hands over his head. "There's one I climb at my mom's house."

She considered him skeptically. Her first impulse was usually to say no. No was safer, easier. But she was in the process of trying to retrain herself. Richard had instructed her on the subject: *The point is to find a way to say yes. Yes instead of no whenever possible.* The tree looked a bit big, but if he climbed at Ruth Ann's house, at school . . . She thought of the cherry tree in her parents' yard, the one she and Peter used to climb until they got too big for it—for the tree or for climbing, she didn't remember which had come first. They used to climb high enough to try to touch the electric wires, believing they might get a shock and wanting to know what that felt like. She supposed that it was in the nature of kids to take risks; learning to say yes must be learning to say yes to risk also. "Okay. I'll boost you to start. But you have to be careful."

"Don't worry."

Ben was getting heavy for carrying over much of a distance, but it was easy enough to hoist him up to the first limb. She shaded her eyes and looked up at him. It was odd to have him towering over her, and yet at the same time he looked small among the bare, arcing branches. Her mind raced back to her own young self, working for footholds on the slippery cherry bark. "Hold on tight. And make sure your foot's solid before you put your weight down on it."

"I *know.*" He was already reaching for the next branch,

and acted as if it were only her talking that was distracting him. "I'm good at climbing."

"Okay. But just take it slow. You've never climbed *this* tree before."

He made no sign that he'd heard her, but shifted himself with what appeared to be care up to his next perch. He held on to the fat, center trunk and worked his way around to another branch the same height, that was a better springboard to the higher rungs. "Jennifer. Look."

"I see you. That's great. How's the view up there?"

"Fine. I'm going to rest here a minute."

"Sounds like a good idea."

Lately, she'd been learning how easy it was to feed him a few encouraging lines that let him believe she was witness, participant—how she could do that and still really be elsewhere, be inside herself, at the same time. Her gaze floated back down to the crocuses and she knelt to them, carefully dug the snow out from around the new leaves. Maybe if these bulbs took hold she'd try some others that would flower in summer, some daylilies. The week before, Richard had brought home a seed catalog, and started talking about planting a vegetable garden out back. He said it would be fun, that the kids would enjoy it. She remembered having to think twice, before the connection seemed natural. Even though she'd been with the kids every weekend for the past six months, even though she was thinking of becoming their stepmother, she still wasn't quite used to planning for a different season and figuring they'd be there, be a part of it.

Of course it wouldn't be that way if the child was her own. Then the other life would stretch forward, inseparable from her own life, and she wouldn't imagine a season without her. Without *her:* Jennifer caught herself. Why, when she thought of having a baby, was the image that came to her automatically one of a daughter? Maybe it was because Richard's children were sons. Maybe it was a tenderness for an image she had of herself as a child, or for that circle of memory that seemed—if she tilted it the right way—to contain only herself and her mother. She pictured the photograph of her mother from her brother's bar mitzvah album, the strapless beaded gown and the pure black curls piled high on her head like a movie star. Then she saw the snapshot of herself at seven or eight that her mother still kept in a chipped gilt frame on her night table. Cranberry velvet dress, starched white collar. Everything precisely in place but the hair that rained down one side of her face, the velvet bow dangling like an apology.

How Marilyn Gold had fussed over Jennifer's hair: forever trying to untangle it, holding it at the roots so the tug of the old metal comb wouldn't hurt so much; every Sunday evening getting out the plastic rollers with their hard teeth and that stinky home permanent, pouring pitcher after pitcher of solution over Jennifer's head, so she'd have banana curls that would last until Tuesday. Jennifer had never understood why her mother got so upset when she'd cut her hair short—her mother who was always urging her to be stylish. "But you had the most beautiful hair." The *had*, in past tense, was drawn out like the syllable of a lament, so much so that you might imagine Jennifer had shaved her scalp clean.

With boys, there were no ribbons and curls, none of that glorious fussing. About the fanciest you got was a new baseball jacket. She looked back across toward the tree, for the square of blue satin. She froze for an instant when she didn't see it. But then the jacket flashed in the sun, farther up. She squinted to make sure she was seeing right. How was it possible? As she'd been daydreaming, he'd worked his way up past where the trunk forked, and out onto a limb that seemed to be swaying and dipping under even his weight. She didn't call out too loudly. She didn't want to surprise him and throw him off balance. "Benjamin!"

He waved one shiny blue arm. "See? I told you."

She stepped slowly toward the base of the tree, as if it were a cat stuck up there and she didn't want to frighten it higher. "Told me what?"

"I could climb good."

"Yeah. Right. Listen, Ben?" She held onto the trunk of the tree and peered up at him, at the legs hanging over the branch. "I think you better come down from there."

"Do I have to?" He craned his neck out to the side to look down at her. The branch crackled.

"Yes, you do. You have to come down." She couldn't believe how measured and firm her voice sounded. "You have to come very carefully."

"All right." Apparently it was the kind of voice that got listened to. "But first call Papa. I want him to see."

"No. It's not a good time now. You're just going to come down, okay?"

It looked from down below as if Ben shrugged his shoulders, and then he started inching backward to the fork of the trunk. "The tree at school's really wicked. It's got this big branch. And there's this kid, Jimmy—"

"Ben."

"Yeah?"

"Just pay attention to what you're doing. Don't talk now."

It seemed to take a long time, but he got back to the trunk and lowered himself with his arms into the crotch between its two forking branches. She wanted to call up directions, to lead him down step by step, but he seemed to know what he was doing. She watched from below as he hesitated before choosing his limb, as he eased himself down from one to another. At a certain point, without even realizing it, she began breathing more easily. He was only about a third of the way up the tree now. She could read the red letters for SLUGGER on the back of his jacket, and she wasn't wearing her lenses. She stepped back from the base of the tree. He would make it. Only those five or six sturdy limbs, like the rungs of a ladder.

Still, she didn't take her eyes off him. She saw his ankle turn on the knot in that branch, only three from the bottom, saw his arms grab for a hold, saw him slip between branches out of the sky.

Everything happened so quickly then: The staccato whimpering, as though he was too scared to scream. The dash to the house to get Richard. *Just come. Now.* The look on Richard's face when he saw the boy lying there, that arm folded up like a wing, and the way he turned to her, as though every trace of love or trust had been drained in that instant with the blood from his face. Before she could think, she was watching him carry Ben into the back of the Honda, watching him run to the house. In what seemed like no time at all, he rushed out with the baby. "Get in. You're driving." He didn't look at her. "We're going to pick Ruth Ann up on the way to the hospital."

"I don't have my lenses in."

"Go grab your glasses or something. Just do it fast. And get a diaper, too, while you're in there."

She practically never wore her eyeglasses, but miraculously she put her hands on them, in her top dresser drawer. She got only the quickest shot of herself in the bathroom mirror, before she grabbed for the diaper and ran. The glasses were small and round, with a plastic tortoise-shell coating over the wire frames. They had the kind of side pieces that curled around her ears, and made her look terribly bookish. She didn't remember until she was out the door with a holler to Jet that she hadn't even washed her face or brushed her teeth yet that morning. She'd just stepped outside in an old sweatshirt and jeans, and discovered the crocuses.

All three of them sat in back. David was strapped in his kids' seat; Richard had Benjamin up on his lap, still whimpering but more softly now. She had to drive quickly but smoothly, so as not to jostle the arm. She'd broken her arm in ninth grade, flying backward off the balance beam on a fancy new dismount. The worst part wasn't the fall itself, or even the moment the doctor twisted the arm to set it right for the cast. It was her mother, driving in her usual heavy-footed style to the doctor's office: too much gas too quickly, too hard on the brake.

Jennifer concentrated closely enough on the driving she almost managed to shut out the thought of Ruth Ann, that Ruth Ann would be getting into the car with them. There was no conversation. Maybe while she'd been in the house Ben had told Richard what he needed to know. *That one branch. That stupid tree, Papa. Jennifer made me come down.* And then there was the rest of the truth, that of course the boy didn't recognize: *Jennifer let me climb too high. She forgot to keep watching me.* In the corner of the rearview mirror she could see Richard, his lips pressed to the top of Ben's head, his eyes turned inward to the circle he made around the hurt boy, as if, even this late, he might shelter him.

She hadn't been in Ruth Ann's neighborhood for a couple of months. Either she didn't drive with Richard to drop the kids off, or she waited somewhere in town, somewhere besides her old corner. Benjamin had been right. The last of the snow had melted here, the lawns were already greening, and almost every house had at least a few crocuses that flashed purple and sunshine as she hurried past them. Ruth Ann was already on the front steps when Jennifer came up the block. She was heading for the curb before Jennifer even pulled over, moving quickly but with a hand pressing into her abdomen. Jennifer had imagined Ruth Ann would sit in the front, but she went for the back door on the driver's side. Richard slid into the middle, toward David's kid's seat, to make room for her.

"Mommy," The word came out small and broken. Benjamin tried to reach out for her but Richard held him, to keep the arm still.

Ruth Ann put her arms around him, there in Richard's lap, so the three of them were locked together, like the parts of one body. "It's okay. Everything's going to be fine. Mommy's here now."

Ruth Ann looked thinner than when Jennifer had seen her last, that day in the restaurant. She was wearing what looked like a new cotton sweater, in a shade of peach that went well with her hair, and her cheekbones were ridged with peach blush. Still, her face looked drawn underneath all that color. Jennifer was suddenly glad for her glasses, glad she looked so sloppy and plain; she hoped Ruth Ann wasn't too caught up to notice.

She hadn't even realized she was craning around, that she'd frozen there, watching them, until Richard barked out the command: "Would you *drive?*"

She snapped her head around forward and lurched too quickly away from the curb. But as she drove she looked at them again in the mirror. Ruth Ann was stroking a finger up and down Benjamin's cheek. Richard had given one hand over to David. They looked so much like a family, the four of them squeezed into her backseat. Jennifer pulled her eyes away from the mirror. She had a job to do and she did it: she drove.

"I called the emergency room." It was Ruth Ann speaking, her voice soft, confidential, as if she didn't want the stranger in the front seat to hear. "The doctor's expecting us."

Richard's voice, adjusted to her timbre: "Good."

"Mommy?"

"Yes, sweetheart."

"Will you and Papa stay with me?"

"Of course we will. We'll be right there with you the whole time."

"Papa?"

"Yes, my brave boy."

"Can we all go back to Mom's house? After it's over?"

Jennifer kept her eyes from the mirror and took in a breath. She knew his *all* did not and could not include her. There was silence until Ben spoke up again, his voice tiny and pitched high with hope. "Can we, Pop?"

Still no answer from Richard.

"Papa."

"Shhh." There was a sound like Richard rubbing Ben's corduroy pants leg. "Quiet now."

At the hospital's emergency entrance, Ruth Ann got out of the car without so much as a glance in Jennifer's direction. She reached in for her son while Richard guided him out. Then Richard followed the two of them onto the curb. He only leaned back in through the door like an afterthought. "Park. And bring in the baby."

Jennifer looked back at David. His blue eyes were round and sober in that chipmunk face. He hadn't cried or fussed the whole ride, as if he'd recognized the emergency, that there was no time for him. Now he hiccupped, and a milky drool ran out of the side of his mouth. She looked around the car for a tissue but didn't find any. She leaned into the backseat and dabbed at his mouth with her sweatshirt sleeve. "It's you and me, kiddo."

She parked and walked back across the lot carrying David, the diaper fluttering in her hand like a signal of distress or surrender. She had tried to move quickly, but already Richard and Ben and Ruth Ann had been taken out of the waiting room. There were a few dozen chairs, only three or four of them filled. There was an old farmer with a thick white stubble over half of his face, his eyes closed to such slits she figured he must have been dozing. A heavyset younger woman had a girl reading a tattered storybook on the floor by her feet. The woman gave Jennifer a knowing, almost conspiratorial smile, which Jennifer was at first too distracted to understand. Then she connected it with the baby squirming around in her arms, grasping the neck of her sweatshirt. She smiled back but vaguely, apologetically.

Along the far wall sat a middle-aged man with the only apparent emergency; he was bleeding through a gauze bandage the length of his forearm. She pulled her eyes away from the stain, the indifferent face. She pictured Benjamin's arm. There hadn't been a spot of blood on it. It had just hung there in the muddied jacket as if it weren't his arm, as if it couldn't be. She remembered the sense she'd had when she'd broken her own, that her body was no longer perfect or whole, that something more basic than bone had been splintered.

It took a minute for the receptionist to look up through her window.

"I'm looking, I mean, I want to inquire about Benjamin Avery. The boy with the arm."

"Mr. and Mrs. Avery went in with him a couple of minutes ago."

She wanted to tell the woman it wasn't *Mr. and Mrs.*

Avery, that, at least as of April eleventh, it wouldn't be. "Is he all right? Can I find out how he's doing?"

"Are you a relative?" The woman's gaze was not suspicious, or accusing, just cold.

Jennifer wasn't a relative; she was just *Jennifer*. She wondered what it would feel like to say, *Yes, I'm his stepmother.* "No. But this is his brother here." She held David forward, as if he were some kind of passport.

"That's fine." The woman was already shuffling files on the counter in front of her. "Why don't you just take a seat? When they come out, I'm sure you'll get all the details."

"How long will that be?"

She didn't even look up this time. "I really can't tell you."

In a few minutes, the man with the bleeding arm got called up and disappeared behind a set of double doors marked NO ENTRANCE. The other man, the woman and child, just sat, as if they weren't actually waiting for anything. The hospital hadn't caught up to the fact that this was a spring morning; the place was still being heated for twenty below. From her neck along her shoulder and down to her chest, she was damp with sweat where David was resting against her, and after a few minutes she realized he'd fallen asleep. The waiting room seemed designed expressly for pacing, with two long aisles running between rows of chairs, but with David sleeping she was stuck in her seat. She kept looking over at the double doors. Wouldn't Richard at least come out for a minute to check on her, to tell her how badly the arm had been broken? She supposed that what she really wanted was to see him apart from Ben and Ruth Ann, to get some sign that he wasn't blaming her.

The doors opened, but it was just the man from before,

coming back to take the same seat, still with the same bloody bandage. She shifted David farther out on her shoulder, so he wasn't drooling right onto her skin. After all, it *wasn't* exactly her fault. He hadn't fallen out of one of the high limbs, the ones she shouldn't have let him climb up to. He'd fallen out of a low one, an easy one; he just hadn't tested his step. Still, by saying he could climb, she'd taken responsibility. It would have been better simply to have said no, always to say no. *Go ask Papa.*

When the doors opened, Ben came out first. The new plaster fairly gleamed in the fluorescent light. The cast looked enormous for a boy of his size; it reminded her of the forearms, like clubs, on his He-Man dolls. It rested across the front of his body, held in a sling, and in his usable hand he carried a big purple lollipop. He waved it when he caught sight of her. His face was streaked with dried tears but now he was smiling.

Richard clamped a hand on his shoulder. "Take it easy, now. Remember what Dr. McAllister told you."

"But I want to show Jennifer."

David stirred on her shoulder when she stood up. She wasn't sure whether Ben wanted to show the cast or the lollipop. Ruth Ann had come up on his other side, as if to protect him, holding the baseball jacket over her arm. Jennifer didn't know where to look. She spoke to no one in particular. "Did it come out a clean break?"

Richard nodded. He looked like he was almost surprised to see her there, her and the baby; as if for the minutes behind those two doors he'd slipped back to an earlier time, when it was just him and Ruth Ann and Benjamin. She stole a look at Ruth Ann, who was keeping her eyes down, refusing to acknowledge the woman holding her baby, covered with her baby's perspiration and drool. But David was reaching out for his mother, as if he would wrestle his way out of Jennifer's arms. She handed the slippery body over to Richard; she tried to meet his eyes but they slid away from hers. Why didn't he or Ruth Ann or both of them turn on her and accuse her? Better that than this silence, for which there was no answer.

The day had turned even warmer while they'd been inside. The sun shimmered off the asphalt, which smelled already like summer. She could feel them walking a few paces behind her, like a different heat at her back. She tried to feel in that heat something like touch, like Richard reaching wordlessly out to her.

The four of them got into the backseat again. Jennifer drove the way she had come, toward Ruth Ann's house, almost as quickly as if there were still an emergency. For the first several blocks no one spoke, but then Ben piped up. "Papa can see my new He-Man fort when we get there. And we can all play." In the mirror she could see the purple head of his lollipop waving.

"Take it easy with that thing." Richard's voice sounded as though he was trying to cover discomfort. "You'll poke somebody's eye out."

"And we can draw stuff on my cast. I've got these great markers now. What are they called again, Mommy?"

"Color Wands."

"Yeah. Color Wands. I've got Color Wands, Papa."

Jennifer downshifted quickly into the red light. She moved her head until she had Richard's face in the mirror, but he was looking off to the side, out the window. Wasn't he going to come out and tell her? Didn't he owe her that? Maybe it had been some kind of bargain. *If you hold still for the doctor, I'll come back to Mom's house. If you let the doctor get a good grip on that arm.* Of course he had every right to go back to Ruth Ann's. His little boy had broken an arm. If all Ben wanted was the solace of both his parents with him under one roof, why deny him that? And yet the arrangement didn't leave very much room for a stepmother.

She pulled slowly away from the light, slowly down the street that led into Ruth Ann's neighborhood. She'd stop in front of the yellow Victorian house and they'd all pile out of the car; she'd be free of them. It was a gorgeous spring Sunday and she'd be free. She could take Jet up the mountain without Benjamin whining to come along with her, and then whining that his legs hurt, couldn't she carry him. She could go visit Pat. She could take herself out for brunch and order whatever she wanted, for herself, without having to share. She could go home and start the poem she'd been thinking about the past week, that spun out from this image of having a daughter. Why was she driving as if she never wanted to get there? Why was she looking backward through her mirror, not for Richard now but for Ben? The flash of grape tongue. The face that looked more and more, the closer they got, as if nothing could hurt him.

CHAPTER 3

It was after nine that evening when she heard the door slam in the driveway and the car pull away. She came out from the study in time to see Jet charging Richard at the door, and Richard pushing the dog away from him. She didn't say anything but just stood, waiting for some apology or explanation. All he offered was, "Hi," tired-sounding but not at all sheepish, as if he spent the better part of every Sunday at Ruth Ann's.

She wanted to give him the same silent treatment he'd given her that morning, but she couldn't help herself. "How's he doing?"

He nodded distractedly, as though Benjamin's arm was no longer the issue. "He's okay. The arm will heal, that's all. Listen."

He turned his eyes on her, soft again, as they hadn't been since he'd first looked at Benjamin on the ground by the tree, and she let out a long breath that felt like it had been pent up all day. It was coming now: he would tell her he understood it wasn't her fault, that accidents happened.

But instead of continuing, he dropped heavily onto the couch and looked down at his hands. "Ruth Ann and I had a talk. About the divorce and all."

She tried to conceal her surprise with a sneer, and made an exaggerated gesture of checking her watch. "Must have been a pretty long talk."

"Give me a break. We didn't start talking until after we put the kids to bed."

"Until after *you* put the kids to bed?" She saw that picture of the perfect family foursome in her backseat. "Is this about you two getting divorced, or your still being married?"

"It's about the divorce. I just told you that."

"Excuse me. The way you make it sound, a person might not be so sure."

"Look, Jennifer. It's been a hard day. Let's not have a big crisis now." He placed his palms together and slid them between his thighs, as if to protect them from weather. "This is the situation: She's going into the hospital in three weeks. Right now is a really hard time for her. She wants to put off the hearing until afterward. Until she's back on her feet."

"So, just put it off?"

"Yeah. That's basically it."

She didn't like the way he wasn't meeting her eyes again. " 'Basically?' "

He stood and buried his hands in his pockets. "There are some things about the agreement she wants to go over. We're going to meet with the lawyers on Wednesday."

"What time Wednesday?"

"Five."

"But that's our movie night." She and Richard had tickets to a French film series at the town library.

"The movie's not until what, six-thirty? We'll make it

in plenty of time. She says it should be just a quick meeting."

"What kinds of things does she want to discuss?"

"Oh, I don't know. We didn't get into specifics tonight. She says it's just some small details."

At six o'clock Wednesday, she let herself into Richard's office with her extra key. He'd said he should be back by six, six-fifteen at the latest. She rarely spent any time in the office, and had never been there by herself. Sitting on the couch, paging through the newspaper, she couldn't shake a sensation of stealth, as if she were trespassing or lying in wait. She'd decided that at twenty past six she'd pin his ticket to the door and go on to the movie without him. At ten after, she wandered from the waiting room couch to his desk, with nothing particular in mind, except having something different to look at.

The walls of his office were covered with color photographs he'd taken on various hikes and canoe trips through Vermont. She'd asked him about some of the shots during their interview the previous spring. She'd used the image of the photographs and the man describing them in the profile she'd written—a vivid way to get across the environmentalist lawyer's passion for nature and his home state. She remembered how the lure of those mountains and rivers had been a part of what drew her to Richard, part of what she'd expected to gain. But they had yet to take a hike, unless she counted walking the trail from the farmhouse; there hadn't been time, between his regular work week and weekends with the kids. As for his famous canoe, it was still in Ruth Ann's garage. The rivers were running now; it must have been about the time of year when he'd taken the picture across from his desk—the bow of his boat pointing up into a stream that looked as swollen and fast as any wild western river. She wondered if the canoe would emerge that spring, or if bringing it out of that shed somehow represented a definitive break with Ruth Ann that he wasn't willing to make yet.

There was a creak like floorboards and her eyes darted up to the doorway, but it was just the building settling, shrinking back as the sun went down. She should have known he'd be late for the movie. She was about to stand up to leave when she noticed the folder headed DIVORCE, at the top of one of his piles of papers.

She looked out again into the lighted reception room, then flipped back the manila cover. Inside was a precisely printed, official document, edged at the top and sides by a pair of pin-fine black lines. Jefferson County Court, October 10, 1985. Plaintiff, Ruth Ann Rosen Avery. It was the agreement, filed with the notice of their separation six months earlier—the agreement that would have been signed into law on April eleventh, that Ruth Ann wanted now to amend.

Jennifer had never seen the actual document, never been particularly interested. She'd seen the hefty check turned over to Ruth Ann on the first of each month, the carved-up visitation calendars. That had always been as much as she'd wanted or needed to know about the bargain Richard had struck with his conscience. And yet if she married him it would be her bargain, too. Maybe some of the details he was meeting with Ruth Ann to discuss should be of concern to her.

When Jennifer heard the sound on the stairs, the digital clock on Richard's bookshelf read 7:18. The room had shadowed with dusk, and she wasn't sure how long it had been since she'd turned the last page. Even when the front door to the office opened, she didn't move to close up the folder and hurry it back to its place.

"Jen?"

"In here."

Richard rushed in with his battered leather portfolio under his arm. "Hey, I'm really sorry it took so long. But look, it's a three-hour movie. We could catch the last two-thirds. I saw it when I was in law school. I'll fill you in on the way over."

He was talking so quickly he didn't seem to notice the dark of the room or the open folder. But then he must have seen the look on her face, and he stopped.

"Fuck the movie."

"Look, I said I was sorry. We could still—"

"That's not it. There's something I think we should talk about."

"Is anything wrong?"

She looked at him and tried to find a handhold somewhere in the shadowed planes of his face, in the patch of forehead that caught the last of the light from the window. Where to begin? It wasn't any particular detail: The monthly payments for the next seventeen years. The doctors' and dentists' bills. The college tuition. The prior consultation if either party should desire to move. The division of Richard's eventual estate . . . It was more the total, cumulative weight of it—the fourteen pages of numbered sections and lettered subparagraphs; this hold that Richard's past exerted over him, reaching forward into the future, even into the grave.

She flipped on his desk lamp and saw him flinch at the glare. The light startled her, too. She placed both hands flat on the opening sheet. "I read the agreement."

He looked down at the paper and then back to her face. "Okay." He dragged the word out, wary, tentative, as if he were waiting to see what would come next.

"No, it's not okay."

He cracked a smile that was nervous with relief. "Hey,

it's not a big deal. So you looked at it. It was sitting right out on my desk. It isn't some classified document. You would have seen it one of these—"

She stared at him until he stopped speaking. "That's not what I mean. It's the agreement itself."

He shifted his portfolio and leaned it on the lip of the desk. "What about it?"

She ran her thumb along the edge of the pages and made a noise like a tiny buzz saw. "Don't you think it's a little . . . severe? I mean, contributing to the support of your children is one thing."

"You know what? Can you do me a favor? I've just been raked over the coals for almost two and a half hours about this agreement. You don't know what you're talking about, okay? And I really don't need any more of it."

She picked up the agreement and stood. "I may not be some big legal expert, but I know what this reads like. It reads like you're shackled to this woman for the rest of your life."

"And aren't I? She's my wife. She's the mother of my two—"

"Ex-wife."

"What?"

"I believe she's your *ex*-wife. Or she's going to be. I seem to recall some discussion about *my* becoming your wife. Unless you've decided to start practicing bigamy."

Richard fell into the chair on the other side of the desk like a much older and heavier man. "Ex-wife. Excuse me. It's been a long evening."

"I can imagine." She tapped the papers against the flat of her hand. "So what is she looking to change?" She sharpened her tone with a sarcastic edge. "I suppose she wants more than this?"

He rubbed his fingers into the skin of his forehead. "That's right. A few minor additions."

"A few minor additions?" She came out from behind the desk and started toward him. "What the hell else can she get? Unless of course you cut off your balls and let her keep them over at her house."

"I'll choose to ignore that remark."

"You can ignore it all you like. You know it's the truth."

"The only thing I know is that unless you calm down, I refuse to continue this discussion."

"Okay, okay, I'm calm." She took a couple of steps back. "So what is she asking for?"

"Sit back down, would you?"

She took the other seat on the client's side of the desk and turned it to face him. "I'm sitting."

"Okay. This is the deal. They wanted to postpone the hearing until after the hysterectomy so she'd still be covered on my medical policy."

She took in and let out a breath. "Okay. That makes sense."

"Right." He unzipped his portfolio and took out a legal pad, covered with notes in his regular but illegible script. "But then her lawyer checked in with some doctors. It seems there are sometimes complications later. Some follow-up visits. Sometimes even some secondary surgery."

"And?"

"And so what they want is a provision that she'll remain on my policy."

"For how long?"

He looked down at the pad, as if he needed to refresh his memory. "Until such time as she chooses to purchase a policy of her own."

"In other words, forever."

"Theoretically."

"So where normally you'd have your wife's name on your policy, you'll have Ruth Ann's. Even if we get married."

"I figured that wasn't a problem. Didn't you tell me you were still listed on your parents' policy?"

"Yeah, right." She could just imagine trying to explain to her father why, even though she was getting married, he shouldn't take her name off his Blue Cross-Blue Shield. "So what else?"

He turned back to his legal pad, and she felt a shade of that sense she'd had in Ruth Ann's living room the previous fall, that she wasn't being spoken to by an actual person. "You saw how the payments were supposed to drop after November, when David turns two? The idea was that it would be easier to get day care then, and she could start working. But her lawyer seems to think it's unclear, after the surgery, how soon she'll be able to do anything more than a real part-time job. So they want the payments to continue at the present level, with an annual cost-of-living adjustment."

She nodded as if that were perfectly reasonable, even though Richard was giving Ruth Ann well over half of his income, before taxes. She didn't want him to get the mistaken impression that it was the money—the precise arithmetic of his generosity—that disturbed her. But she couldn't help picturing Ruth Ann in her lawyer's office, in a fancy new sweater, pressing her hand into her abdomen and putting on a dramatic, pained look. Jennifer felt bad about the hysterectomy, too, but it wasn't exactly a lifetime disability.

"One more thing."

"What's that?"

"Life insurance."

"What about it?"

"I'm supposed to take out a policy. With her as the beneficiary."

"So, when you die, she'll be just like your widow. I mean, she's already down for twenty percent of your will."

"The will is one thing. This is different. This is like if I were to die prematurely, when she was still dependent on me for supporting the kids."

"So she's placing a bet and you're paying the tab. She's gambling on your life, and you're paying."

He stood up and put the pad back into his portfolio, as if he were ready to leave. "I know you're all worked up over this, but you don't understand. If I drop dead, she's left alone with two kids. Do you have any idea what that's like? She's got to have some security."

He turned toward the door, but she grabbed hold of his arm, and spun him back around, facing her. "You're right. I don't understand. I don't have any idea what it's like. So I guess that means it's none of my business. You've asked me to marry you. Now you're signing your life away, but I get no say in the matter."

"I'm not signing my life away. But anyway, I don't have much say in the matter myself."

"What does that mean?"

He put the portfolio back on the desk. "Look, we listened to everything they had to say. Then I went back with my lawyer to his office. And I asked him. I said, 'Look, John, do I have to go along with this?' "

She eased herself back down into her seat. "So what did he say?"

"He said I didn't have very much room to maneuver."

"Maybe you need a new lawyer."

"There *are* no new lawyers." He started pacing between the desk and the wall. "There are two reputable divorce attorneys in this whole town. She's got one and I've got the other. Look, I've known John for ten years. He sat me down and put his hand on my shoulder. You know what he said to me? 'Face it, man. You start carrying on an affair. You walk out on a wife with an infant and a four-year-old kid. You're living openly for eight months with this other woman. Your wife's going into the hospital for a full hysterectomy. You're not poor. Even if you did try to fight it, you think you've got a chance in the world to get a judge's sympathy?' "

She swallowed against a knot of doom rising up in her throat—the same feeling that had settled over her reading the papers, only stronger now.

"You know what else he said?"

She gave the obligatory, slow shake of her head.

"He said that even if I got lucky—even if I got one of the liberal judges on the rotation—I wouldn't be winning. Not if I wanted to hold up my head. Not if I wanted to stay and practice law in this county."

She stood up. Behind the windowpanes the night was deep blue; there was no hope of salvaging even the final third of the movie. "You and Ruth Ann could have saved yourselves a few bills, and just hired one lawyer."

He tilted his head and raised his eyebrows. "We live in a small town, my love."

She reached across the desk to flip off the light. "I'm just beginning to realize how small."

CHAPTER 4

Ruth Ann drove with a friend down to Boston on Monday, the third week in April. She was admitted to the hospital that afternoon; the hysterectomy was to be performed Tuesday morning. That day, before dawn, something woke Jennifer. When she opened her eyes she expected Benjamin at the side of the bed, but it was Richard, sitting bolt upright, his pillow balled tight in his lap. He spoke without looking straight at her, as if they were in the middle of a conversation. "What if she dies?"

She rubbed her eyes. "What?" As soon as she'd said the word, his question came clear to her.

"She could die, you know."

She sat up and found his hand in the fist of the pillow. "Hey. Come on." She couldn't help shaking her head. "It's a routine operation. She's not going to *die* from it."

But he wasn't shrugging it off. His profile had a carved, insomniac intensity. "You get into a hospital, they cut you open—anything's possible."

She scratched her scalp to wake up more. "She could also die driving Ben to his school." She searched her hazy brain for an example that was less typical, more to the point. "She could have died during childbirth."

"She almost did."

"You're kidding." Either she was used to the dark or some light had started to leak through the window; she could see him more plainly now. His face had not looked this drawn since the day he'd first heard about the hysterectomy. "You never told me that."

"Yeah." He squeezed his hand deeper into the pillow, until she couldn't keep hold of it. "It was the first time, with Ben. It was my own stupidity. We had a home birth. I hadn't wanted to do the home thing at first, but Ruth Ann convinced me. And then I got into it. Everything was going just fine, but then she retained her placenta. The midwife said we could go to the hospital right away, or we could wait half an hour, to see if it would come out on its own. Like idiots we decided to wait."

"So what happened?"

"So what happened was that by the time we got the ambulance and got her over there, she was really weak and she'd lost a shitload of blood. And they had to extract the placenta manually. I'll never forget it. The doctor looked at me like I was some kind of murderer. *Five more minutes and she might not have made it.* That's what he said to me."

She looked at his eyes, expecting to see tears, but they were perfectly dry.

"That was the start of all this. The doctore told her the day he was letting her out: another pregnancy and she might be asking for trouble.

"I used to think about it a lot, when things got bad with her. What it would have been like if she'd died. If it had been just me and the baby. Sometimes I really wished it, I swear. I know it sounds terrible."

"It's okay."

He shook his head. "No, it's not okay, but it's true. Sometimes I even catch myself wishing it lately. Like when I'm missing the kids. Not that she'd die, exactly—just disappear. Just take off somewhere."

She was surprised to hear him saying this, he who seemed these days to bear such good will toward Ruth Ann—surprised to hear him echo her own secret wishes. How many times since the night she'd read the agreement had she caught herself at those morbid fantasies? But there was a difference. For Richard, getting rid of Ruth Ann was just a way to get David and Benjamin, to have them there *all the time*. That was the last thing Jennifer wanted. It was bad enough they'd be here for two solid weeks while Ruth Ann recovered from the hysterectomy.

What Jennifer wanted was Richard, all to herself. To satisfy her, Ruth Ann couldn't just vanish alone; the kids would have to vanish along with her.

She slid back down in the bed and turned over, away from him. "But she's not—disappearing."

Of course Ruth Ann wasn't going to die. Still, Jennifer couldn't help feeling relieved Tuesday night when the call came—relieved at the rhythm, steady but feeble, leaking out of the receiver around Richard's ear. The next morning, Richard set Benjamin up on the phone with his mother. Richard and Ruth Ann had decided that putting David on was too risky; hearing her, he'd probably start missing her, and that would mean trouble. So Jennifer kept him upstairs an extra long time in the tub, letting him splash until the floor was shiny with bathwater. His favorite bathtub toy was a blue plastic cube with holes in the bottom. She dunked it under, then held it up in the air, so the water rained out the holes. David shook his head back and forth and pointed at the trickling. "Pee-pee."

Downstairs, Ben had finished his phone call, and Richard was fixing peanut butter and honey sandwiches. She set David up in his high chair and then went back to the living room doorway.

Ben was busy with a pile of his He-Man guys, rattling off a high-pitched monologue, the way he usually did when deep in his play. The bulk of the monologue was always a mindless, violent litany: *I'll smash you. No, take that. This guy's dead. No, he isn't.* But sometimes, if she listened carefully and for long enough, she'd pick up a strain of something important to Benjamin. *I did not hurt my brother. Go take time out in your room. You can go back to your mom's house now.*

He didn't seem to have noticed her, so she stayed just inside the doorway. With the cast on his right arm, he could only play with his left hand. He was taking one of the men and hitting it into another one laid out on the carpet.

"Ouch. That hurts."

"You bet it does. See how you like this karate kick."

"I'll kill you."

"You won't kill me. I have my whole army."

She was about to give up on her eavesdropping and go help Richard, but then Ben shifted to a different part of the rug. He already had another little scene going there, with a new set of figures from *Star Wars* Richard had given him Monday. The figure of Princess Lea was splayed out, with a tiny, camouflage-patterned robe laid on top of her. She was surrounded by a circle of alien warriors.

"Please." Ben made his voice higher than usual. "Don't cut into my tummy."

"But we have to."

"Oh, no. Someone save me."

He reached back to his other pile and extracted one of the jumbo-size He-Men. He didn't say anything; he just took the big figure and started bashing the miniature aliens down. He kept it up until Richard called him for breakfast.

She let him squeeze past her and stayed in the doorway, looking back at his battleground, seeing the ferocity of his small, hero's face. His fantasy had an integrity that adult daydreams tended to lack. He was saving his mother; it was as simple as that. She thought about the secret desire Richard had voiced last night, and her own, unspoken one—their basic dishonesty. What made the man imagine that his sons would be anything but miserable if they lost Ruth Ann? And how did Jennifer think she could make Richard happy, taking his children away from him?

"Jennifer?"

"Hmmm."

"Do you still have your you-tis?"

It was Thursday, late afternoon. She'd decided to take Ben for a hike through the woods, as a way to distract him and tire him out; he hadn't been sleeping very well since Ruth Ann had gone into the hospital. A week ago there had still been only buds, but now the leaves had opened into an airy, dappling canopy; underfoot, the path was carpeted with tiny wild strawberry blossoms and purple dog violets, so thickly there was no choice but to trample them.

"Do I still have my what?"

"Your you-tis. You know. Your utis." He was flustered, the way he sometimes got when he couldn't make himself clear, and acted as if it were *her* fault, or Richard's; he almost looked as if he might start to cry if he had to repeat it again.

She thought for a moment and then it came to her. "You mean my uterus?"

"Yeah. That's it. Uterus. Do you still have yours?"

Jennifer knew that Ruth Ann had explained to Ben about why she was going into the hospital; she'd heard Richard say things like, "When Mom gets her tummy fixed." But she'd had no idea Ruth Ann had gone so far as to use the word *uterus* with a five-year-old—to tell him she was having her uterus taken out. In her effort to make the procedure sound absolutely routine, she seemed to have given him the impression that a uterus was something some women kept and some women didn't—like people either did or didn't still have their tonsils or wisdom teeth. "Yes, I still have my uterus."

"My mom doesn't." He said this almost as if it were a matter of pride.

"I know."

"She told you?" He tripped over a root sticking up in the path, hobbled along a few steps but then regained his footing.

"She didn't tell me personally, no. But I know that's why she went to the hospital."

"Yeah." He sounded offhand, smug, in the knowledge. "That's why she went." He picked up a stick from the side of the path and wielded it like a sword in front of him. "Does your uterus hurt you?"

"Hurt me? No." He seemed to be building up to his usual comparison between the two women; she didn't doubt that before he was done, she'd be made to seem somehow inadequate because she wasn't having a hysterectomy, and his mother had had one.

But he went quiet, and they just walked. She was glad he wasn't yet saying he was tired, that they had to turn back. This was the farthest he'd ever walked down the trail. He was five and a half now; in September, he'd be starting first grade. His legs were already long for a boy of his age, smooth with muscle. Every couple of minutes Jet barreled down the trail out of nowhere, or cut them off

216

from the side, where he'd forayed into the woods. She remembered last fall, the first times they'd taken Ben walking, the way he'd shrieked and clung to Richard's side whenever the dog galloped by. Now he stood his ground, or stepped off to the edge of the trail, to let Jet run through without hurting him.

Finally Ben seemed to take stock of the distance they'd traveled. "Is this still the same trail?" His breathing was labored, and she realized she'd probably been walking too fast for him.

"Same trail, all right. Just the woods has changed." It was cooler and shadowed under what was now mostly pines; the wildflowers had given way to low moss and a spongy sediment of old needles.

"Can we take a rest?" He stooped over, leaning on his stick as if it were a cane.

"Sure. Let's rest. And then we'll head back. We've got to walk all that same way again, you know."

He nodded and looked up at her from his bent position. It seemed more that he was hyperventilating, on purpose, than panting from his exertion. "If you don't have a uterus, you can't have a baby."

She looked at him for a moment and then said it slowly: "That's true."

"So my mom can't have any." He was standing now, cradling his cast with his good hand, as if suddenly the weight were a burden. He'd changed his mind about letting anyone draw on the cast; he'd decided he wanted it white. Now it was soiled to an undistinguished gray, the color of dried summer dirt.

"But she doesn't need to." She tried to sound bright. "She's got you and David already. Two's enough, don't you think? My mother only had two. She stopped after two, because that's all she wanted."

"And she still had her uterus?"

"Yup."

He seemed to be chewing that over.

"You want to walk back now?"

"Okay." But after a few steps he stopped again. "Since you have your uterus, why don't you have one?"

"A baby?"

"Yeah."

"Maybe someday I will." She started walking again so he would follow her lead, only slowly.

"If you did, would it be my brother?"

"Maybe. Your half brother. Or half sister." *Maybe.*

"Would it go back and forth between here and my mom's house?" He didn't seem to be taking the *maybe* into account.

"No. It would just be here, with me and your dad." *If your dad were the father.*

He swung his stick at a maple sapling. "Wouldn't it go to Mom's house *sometimes*? Like when you and Papa had to go on a trip?"

She knew that taken more lightly, it would be funny, or cute—this confusion—but she couldn't help shuddering at the image of her child being tied even remotely into this life of joint custody. "I guess if we went on a trip, we'd take the baby along with us."

He shrugged and whipped his stick at the side of the trail again, as if the whole constellation of arrangements were too complex for him. "So when are you going to have it?"

It was strange, to have this thing she'd only imagined, only seen on the level of a secret and somewhat distant desire, being insisted on—and by Benjamin, of all people. "Oh, not for a while. If I even do." The idea suddenly took on the shape of a burden, the way she imagined it might seem to Richard. "Your dad and I would have to discuss it."

"Doesn't he want one?" The question came out as if for Richard *not* to would be an affront, a statement about Ben and David.

"I don't know if he'd want one or not." She tried to make it sound casual. She rested a hand on his shoulder, then let it slide down. "He's already got two such good boys."

CHAPTER 5

When the phone rang, Jennifer had just finished squeezing a balanced meal into Ben's *Masters of the Universe* lunch box. Richard was spooning applesauce into David, faster than the boy could swallow it, so it was oozing from his lips and dribbling down to his chin. Richard had to drop the kids off by eight-thirty—Ben at school, David at the sitter's—so he could get to a ten o'clock hearing on the other side of the state. The last thing they needed now was a phone call.

The second ring sounded jangling, insistent. She grabbed the phone before it went off a third time. "Hello?"

"This is Ruth Ann." The voice came through faint, as if she were calling long distance from some remote outpost. "Please put Richard on."

"Just a second." Jennifer kept the phone to her mouth, as if she might say something more. Ruth Ann had been home from the hospital for a few days, she'd called a number of times, but Jennifer had never managed anything beyond the usual, perfunctory, *okay, hold on* variations. She did want to say something, but when she tried to figure out *what*, the particular words got lost in a tangle of anger and sympathy.

But this would not be her moment. Richard had already jumped up and was reaching for the phone. He mouthed, "Ruth Ann?" and she nodded. As he took the receiver, he motioned her back to the table, where David sat with his applesauce. "Hi. Listen, I've got to make it a fast one. I'm running late for a hearing date down in Bennington."

Jennifer scooped some applesauce into the spoon, but froze with it before she reached David's mouth; she was watching Richard's face, trying to guess at what Ruth Ann was saying.

"Sorry. I can't today. As it is I'll be lucky if I get to this hearing. Look, there's got to be somebody else you can call."

Jennifer set the spoon down in the dish and stood up.

"I know your friends work. So do I. You'll just have to—"

"Richard?"

He waved her off with an impatient flick of his wrist.

But she walked toward him. In the past weeks, along with fantasizing about the other woman's demise, Jennifer had dreamed up any number of scenes where she confronted Ruth Ann about the agreement. Maybe this was her opening, the chance she never imagined she'd actually have. "What does she need?"

He brought the phone away from his face and looked at her quizzically.

She repeated it: "What does she need? I'm going to be home all day with a car. I could help her."

He didn't take his eyes off her as he brought the receiver back to his lips. "Did you hear that?"

She was close enough to him now to hear the silence over the line.

"I said, 'Did you hear that?' Jennifer's got a car and she's going to be home today. She'd be happy to pick up what you need."

Still there was silence. Richard was squinting his eyes at her as if, even as she watched, his surprise were being taken over by tenderness. He must imagine he knew what this meant: that Jennifer was ready to work toward a rapprochement. It was almost as if he were squinting at the vision of a peaceable constellation, in which his ex-wife and his new wife would be fixed about him. She herself had a different idea, which was coming clearer to her now, as they waited.

Finally the words sounded through the receiver, a stingy "All right."

Richard raised both his eyebrows and sucked in a breath, as if the concession were fragile. Jennifer's ear was practically sharing the receiver with his; she could hear Ruth Ann perfectly: "There are a couple of refill prescriptions ready at Wright's. And I need a bottle of vitamin E oil. I'll call ahead to tell them to okay a charge. The front door will be open. I'll be upstairs in bed. Tell her to just come in and put the stuff down in the kitchen."

The sky had been clear at the farmhouse, but as she drove down the three-mile hill she descended into a bank of fog that hadn't yet burned off the river. By the time she reached town, the car was moving through a watery mist that seemed to cling to the buildings. In this viscous light, Ruth Ann's house looked paler than Jennifer had remembered it, almost the color of eggshells. From across the street, she could see that behind the curtains most of the shutters were drawn; the place definitely had the look of a house where someone was sick. She had a vague memory of her grandmother's house, a Victorian also, on a neat little block, the last few times her parents brought her to visit—the way, even at her age, even knowing nothing of death, she sensed that she shouldn't touch anything, that she should smile but not speak.

She walked up the path slowly, wondering if Ruth Ann had already heard her, or if she were sleeping. Jennifer knew she was supposed to just open the door. She wouldn't be ringing and waiting, as she'd done the past fall, as she'd done so many times in her dream. Still, she hesitated on the porch without touching the doorknob. It occurred to her that she'd stopped having that old, wishful dream about Ruth Ann's welcome. And yet her dreams hadn't stopped bringing her to this door. Now sometimes she was marrying Richard, the morning of the wedding had come, only she realized he hadn't gotten divorced yet. For some reason it was her job, and not his, to go to Ruth Ann and ask her for the divorce. There Jennifer would be, at this door, all dressed up in some hopeful bridal confection, panicked at the thought of everyone waiting for her at the temple—Richard, her parents, the bridesmaids—but Ruth Ann wasn't home, or she was refusing to answer.

Today, Ruth Ann would not have a choice. Jennifer could just walk in the door; she knew where to find her. And wasn't this what Jennifer had in mind now: to ask the other woman for a divorce? Not the kind Ruth Ann intended to extract, but a real one—a divorce that would set Richard, at least in some measure, free.

When she finally pushed, the door didn't give. Maybe Ruth Ann had forgotten to open it, and Jennifer *would* have to ring. She turned sideways and gave a sharp ram with her shoulder and hip, and practically went tumbling into Ruth Ann's front hallway. She got her footing and took in a breath. It wasn't exactly the entrance that she had intended. Even if Ruth Ann had been napping, she was certainly awake now. It must have sounded as if

someone were breaking her door down. Jennifer's eye
traveled up along the heavy maple banister. She didn't see
a light seeping down from the bedrooms; the upstairs
landing seemed to dissolve into its own darkened mist.
And yet of course Ruth Ann was up there, touching her
hand to an abdomen that didn't feel like her own, that felt
so hard and, inside, strangely weightless. Listening for the
sounds of Jennifer in the hall, Jennifer moving back toward the kitchen; listening most of all for the moment the
front door would close safely behind her.

Jennifer carried the pharmacy bag to the kitchen and
set it onto the table. Now she was supposed to turn
around; her task was accomplished. She stopped and listened a moment; the air in the house was heavy but there
was no sound. She let her eyes roam the kitchen. There
was a dish drainer next to the sink, filled with a few plates
and mugs from the meager fare of convalescence and
solitude. There was a countertop lined along its whole
length with cookbooks, for the exquisitely competent
mother and, formerly, wife. On the refrigerator were
snapshots of the two children. Jennifer's eye was drawn to
a baby picture of Benjamin, sitting in a red wagon. What
struck her was how his face looked the same, as if it had
already been perfectly formed and finalized long before
she'd ever laid eyes on him. When she looked at the picture more closely, she noticed the wagon's handle, ex-
tending out past the frame. Someone had been pulling it,
probably Richard. Ruth Ann had cut him out of the shot,
and yet in the tension of the handle she still had him
there, holding up his end, effective, invisible.

She walked back to the table and lifted the items out of
the bag. She took a mug from the dish drainer and filled
it with water. She could carry the mug in one hand, the
bottles of pills and the oil in the other. At the foot of the
stairs she paused, wondering if she should call up some

warning, but she kept her silence, and even took the steps on tiptoe, as if she were sneaking up on somebody. She stopped at the landing. Which of the doors was Ruth Ann's? There was one to the right, that was closed, and a few more down the hall away from the street. It was from that direction the voice came.

"Do me a favor, why don't you?"

She could tell it was a strain for Ruth Ann to be speaking this loudly.

"I asked you to just leave it downstairs."

Jennifer walked toward the voice that sounded as if it had come from the middle bedroom. "I've got your pills and some water."

No answer.

She waited in front of the door for a moment. "I'm going to come in."

She worked the hand that was holding the bottles onto the doorknob. Without dropping the bottles, she could only turn the knob slowly. Once the door was open, she was surprised at the light coming in from the opposite window, as if the fog outside had started to burn. The bedroom wasn't terribly large, or at least it didn't seem large, with the king-sized bed filling it.

Ruth Ann sat up against a couple of pillows, at one edge of the bed. Jennifer wasn't sure of her expression at first, the way the misted glare came in from behind her, like a backlighted photograph.

"I wanted to talk to you."

Ruth Ann closed the thick paperback book in her lap. She looked at Jennifer with a set of the face that was coming clearer now, that was hard. "As long as you've barged in here, why don't you bring me that medicine?"

Jennifer didn't like Ruth Ann's tone, but she supposed she'd asked for it. She walked around the bed and set the mug and bottles onto the night table. She took a few steps back, and watched Ruth Ann bend stiffly, painfully, to reach the water and pills. It was with some difficulty that she opened the bottles, and swallowed two pills from each one. Only when she was settled back against the headboard did she look up at Jennifer. "So what was it you wanted to talk about?"

Part of Jennifer wanted to abandon her plan, to wish Ruth Ann well, and disappear from the bedroom. But she'd come this far, and she didn't want the kind of regrets she'd suffered after their meeting last fall. She wasn't going to get another chance like this. "It's about the divorce. The agreement."

Just for an instant, Ruth Ann's expression flickered surprise, but that was quickly covered by a look of unconcern Jennifer couldn't help reading as haughty. "What about it? What business is it of yours?"

Jennifer took a deep breath. "It's very much my business. Richard has asked me to marry him."

She was counting on that announcement to work some dramatic effect, but Ruth Ann just held her lips in a line and smoothed the blanket over her midsection. "Yes, well. I suppose that was to be expected." She said this with a complete and irritating placidity, as if the issue were of as little consequence as a change of address, or a haircut.

"Look. You can make light of it if you want to. But it's important to Richard. It could be important for your two children." In the fever of making her point, she allowed herself to take some liberties with the truth. "He wants to start a new life. Maybe start a new family."

Even that assertion didn't seem to ruffle Ruth Ann. It dawned on Jennifer that this tranquillity in the face of a showdown was entirely unnatural; that the bottles of pills she'd brought from the pharmacy must have been painkillers. "That's all well and good. The best of luck to you."

Ruth Ann leaned across to the night table with her earlier stiffness and took a sip of the water. Jennifer thought that was all she was going to say, but then Ruth Ann surprised her: "That doesn't cancel out his responsibilities to his first family."

Maybe it was the pills again that made Ruth Ann speak so slowly, but the way she said those two words—*first family*—she sounded like a junior-high teacher, introducing a term in basic civics or ethics. Divorce notwithstanding, Ruth Ann would always be Richard's *first wife*, Ben and David his original children. Whatever family Jennifer might hope to have with him would be *second*, with all that position implied. Second string. Second fiddle. Second priority.

"Can't you cut him some slack?" Jennifer could hear the pleading tone in her voice; she raised her volume to cover it. "He made a mistake, okay? Do you have to take his whole life for it?"

In the silence that followed her outburst, Jennifer could hear the futility of her own words, like a flattening echo. Of course Ruth Ann was going to take his whole life, if he let her, if he didn't fight for it. What had ever made her think appealing to Ruth Ann would make any difference? Jennifer waited for the other woman to tell her that in so many words; to tell her she was entitled to whatever she was getting, and more.

But Ruth Ann didn't say anything right away, as if she were letting the last of the echo die in the air, and do her work for her. When she spoke, her words came out weak, but with a new edge to them. "If you don't mind, I need to get across the hall to the bathroom."

Jennifer stared at her. She wasn't exactly sure what the woman was asking.

Ruth Ann's voice sounded more pinched and commanding. "I need you to come to the side of the bed."

Jennifer froze. She'd come here to fight, not play nurse-maid.

When Jennifer didn't move, Ruth Ann drew back her blanket and swung her legs slowly around to the floor. She was wearing a flower-print nightgown, sheer enough that Jennifer could see the outline of the tube and the bag, even while Ruth Ann was still sitting.

It was like that moment last fall, when Ruth Ann had caught Jennifer's expression before she could hide it. Once again Jennifer had the sense that out of some perversity, Ruth Ann was pleased—this time even in spite of her pain: pleased with the way her affliction seemed to set her beyond any argument or reproach the other woman might muster. And indeed, she wasn't entirely wrong in this. How could Jennifer fight with a woman who couldn't stand up and go to the bathroom? How could she hope to win anything, when her opponent's loss of dignity was, by implication, her own?

Jennifer could barely look at her. "I'm sorry. I didn't realize—" She stepped toward the bed and woodenly put out an arm.

Ruth Ann rested both hands on it, and Jennifer lifted. Once she was standing, Ruth Ann hung her arm over Jennifer's shoulder and leaned down hard. "It sounds to me like you've got a problem." Now that her weight was on Jennifer, Ruth Ann's voice had gone calm again, even superior. "But I'm not the person you should be speaking to."

CHAPTER 6

She thought she could put the question off until Sunday, when the kids would be back at Ruth Ann's. But Saturday morning the longer light woke her early, and she sat up in bed looking at Richard, the inscrutable laxity of his mouth in sleep, until it came clear to her: to look at him was to fall more deeply in love with him. She couldn't afford to do that for even another few minutes without knowing the answer.

When she whispered his name, he turned over, as if carrying the syllables off with him into some dream. She whispered again and pushed at his arm, and his eyes opened. They were unfocused a moment, then sharpened with an instinctive alarm: "Is the baby up?"

"No. It isn't the baby."

"What time is it?"

"Twenty to six."

"Jesus." His head fell back onto the pillow. "Then come down and cuddle me."

He didn't wait for her to lie back down in bed. He circled her belly and lower back with his arms and nuzzled into her bare hip, seeming for a moment to be sleeping again, but then coming to life as he started to kiss her. "I get the idea." He dove back down for a bite at her waist. "You didn't want to wait till tomorrow."

Waiting till tomorrow meant waiting till the kids were back at Ruth Ann's; waiting to resume the pleasure Jennifer and Richard usually took in their morning lovemaking. And he had a point. It was early enough they could probably get away with it.

But she couldn't. "Stop, okay?" One of his hands was working at parting her thighs. "I've got something to ask you."

He retreated from his embraces and looked sideways up at her, disappointed, even suspicious, as if it were going to be about Ruth Ann, about the agreement. "What's that?"

"I wondered what you thought about you and me having a baby."

When she'd pictured herself asking the question, she'd imagined a couple of scenarios for the response. In one, he looked sorry and businesslike and shook his head *no* several times. He already had two children, which was as much as anyone should be entitled to bring into the world these days. He had this enormous emotional and fiscal responsibility. He could not in good conscience extend that commitment. In the other, a smile dawned slowly but brilliantly on his face as he looked at her. He hadn't wanted to scare her by bringing the idea up himself; he'd figured she was nowhere near ready. But there was nothing in the world that would make him happier.

That's how she'd pictured it—an unequivocal yes or no, like the flip of a coin, neatly deciding her future. She'd never considered this possibility: The question took a moment to register, and when it did, he continued to

look at her blankly. "A baby? The two of *us*?" Plainly the
notion had never occurred to him.

"That's what I said. I think we're the only two in here."
She cast a glance down at Jet on the rug, in his most
vulnerable, spread-legged position, at the acorn of extra
black fur from what had been his scrotum. "The only two
still capable."

"Very funny."

"Well, then . . ." She still had a chance. Okay, so it
hadn't occurred to him. But now that the idea had been
advanced, he might warm to it, might realize the foolish-
ness of his previous oversight. She watched his face
closely for the birth of that willingness, but instead saw a
drawing together of eyebrows, like incomprehension, like
anger.

"Look. Jennifer. It's not even six o'clock on a Saturday
morning. Ruth Ann's just out of the hospital from a hysterectomy. David'll be running around in diapers for another good year. You've never even told me you'd marry
me. You have to start asking me *now* about having a child
with you?"

"When would you like me to ask?"

"In four or five years maybe." He smiled weakly, after
the fact, as if he'd intended some irony.

"I'm not sure it can wait that long."

"Oh, it can wait. If you keep it in shape." He moved
over next to her. "I'm not *that* old, you know."

She wanted to say, *And I'm not that young.* She didn't
want the scene turning playful. She wanted to give him
one more chance to say yes. Yes sincerely. Not right now,
but in a couple of years. That will be part of our marriage.

But his head was under the covers now, he was moving
up her legs with his hands and his tongue, and that was
just as well, because this way he couldn't look at her face.

Five years down the line, who could say what he'd decide? There were no guarantees; he wasn't offering any. The only sure thing was that he wanted a wife, a woman to be his boys' stepmother.

She wouldn't tell him this morning. She wouldn't tell him until after he signed the divorce papers. This was not going to be one more in that complex of pressures. But she knew now. And how strange it was the way all his coaxing touches seemed both more simply of the flesh and more abstract, now that she did—as if she were not so much feeling them as already trying to fix them in memory.

She would have liked to stay home, but there was no ready excuse. Starting at eleven o'clock, the high school a few towns over was holding a carnival. Earlier that week, Richard had spotted the ad in the local newspaper, and they'd decided it would make a good treat for the boys' final day with them. Backing out now would seem strange, and there wouldn't be too many more chances like this, to be with Ben and David. Have fun with them.

They were all in the Honda, ready to go to the fair, when she remembered the bag, with the kids' sun hats and David's diapers and bottle. The phone was ringing as she walked back in the door, but she let the machine take it.

"It's your mother. It's Saturday morning. Just calling to see how you are." Marilyn paused but she didn't hang up, as if she suspected her daughter were really there, listening; as if, in that moment of recorded silence, the two might feel somehow closer.

Jennifer pictured a Saturday morning in June, when Marilyn would call and it would just be Jennifer and Jet alone in the house again. Jennifer would say everything was fine, the way she always did. Maybe she'd make some offhand remark about how things hadn't worked out with that lawyer. It would be as if her life had circled in on itself, swallowing her year with Richard, her months with the boys; as if she hadn't almost *married* somebody.

Jet stood by the phone machine, cocking his head to the click and whir of the tape as if it were some living creature. When the sounds stopped, he circled twice and settled onto the floor. His brown eyes rose to hers with a look that her mother, when she'd seen the dog, had mistaken for sadness, but which Jennifer knew was serenity. What could a dog understand about vows—about *only*, *forever*? *Only* was the one you were with; *forever* must be the timeless moment in which you were waiting.

The fair was set up in the high-school parking lot. From a distance, it was one crazy mass of color and motion. David clung to her neck, his eyes gone glassy, enormous, not sure yet if the sight were terrifying or wonderful. As they got closer, she could see that the front of the lot was given over to booths, with games and refreshments. Clowns strolled the aisles with great rainbow bouquets of balloons, and already the sky was dotted with tiny, receding circles of color. At the rear of the lot were the rides. From the entrance, she could only see three: a teacup ride, a contraption with short, waving arms like an octopus, and, all the way to the back, towering over the others, a Ferris wheel.

Ben had stopped by the ticket booth, and he seemed to be looking up at it, too.

Jennifer caught up to him before Richard did. "You want to go on the Ferris wheel first?"

He stood up on tiptoe as if that would really give him a much better view. "Yeah. Once we get cotton candy."

Richard came up in time to hear that, and he gave her the eye. He and Ruth Ann didn't like the kids to eat junk food. But that morning, while Richard was giving David a bath, Jennifer had told Ben about the carnival and all the things they might do there. She'd told him about a carnival at her own grade school, where the parents had been enlisted to help, and her mother had run the cotton candy drum—how she and her brother had spent most of the day watching the tiny sugar filaments magically appearing and wrapping like fairy hair around the white cardboard cones; how sick they'd gotten from eating all the ones that came out too short or too lopsided.

She shrugged at Richard. It was easy to spoil children if you were passing out of their lives, easy to hope they might take away that sweet memory. "Just this once. Just a small one. I promised him."

At the cotton candy booth, David started to cry. Richard leaned across her to put his hands over the baby's ears. "It's the noise of that drum, I think. That screeching sound."

She shook her head. "I think the thing is he wants one."

As if to prove her right, David ducked free of Richard's hands and reached for the rack of gossamer spools.

She brought him almost close enough to touch them. "You want one, too, don't you?"

Ben left the booth holding up the pink mass as if it were a prize he'd earned at one of the tossing or shooting games. David waved his around like a wand, and she didn't snap at him when it caught in her hair. She pulled a strand off to taste it. She'd forgotten it was that grainy, that strong, that it would dissolve in her mouth this way.

From halfway across the lot came the pulsing, tinsel, Ferris wheel music. They waited on line, but when they got to the front, there was only one car left, and the attendant said Ben was too big to sit up on one of their laps. That meant it had to be the two kids, and either Richard or Jennifer. Richard's mouth opened, as if he were making a quick, last-ditch calculation, as if there were some possible compromise.

But she could see Ben moving close in to his father's side. She took a step away from the entrance gate. "You guys go."

Richard's eyes looked sorry when he turned to her. "We'll wait on line again after, so you can go up with them."

She handed David over and ducked from a sideways jab of his cotton candy. "It's okay. I'll watch." Then she remembered the camera that she'd stuck at the last minute into the diaper bag; she'd realized that with her whole wall of snapshots, she didn't have even one of the three of them. "I'll take your picture."

Once he had Richard and the two boys strapped into their seats, the attendant moved toward the center base of the wheel, where he worked the control lever. She walked back a few paces, to the edge of a cluster of mothers and fathers who were calling out and waving, their eyes on the wheel; one woman was frantically throwing kisses, as if at an airport or train station. When Jennifer looked back up, the wheel had started to turn. For a moment she didn't spot them. But there they were, almost rounding the top. They slipped over and disappeared down the far side. When they swung back around the bottom of the wheel she was ready.

Ben! David! Richard! Did she actually shout it? She must have. They saw her, and their mouths opened in one unanimous vowel that arced out and got lost in the music, the turning. Now they spun faster, and with each revolution, something like acceptance turned until it found its place in her: They only swung toward her to slip away; reached out their arms as if only to prove that they couldn't pull her up with them.

When the ride had started to slow again, she thought of

the camera. It took a few turns of the wheel to steady it, to focus on that part of the arc where they first pitched and swung toward her. She let the other cars, the faces, slide in and out of the frame. They must have rounded the top by now; they must be on their way down. The wheel was moving slowly enough this could be her last chance. She took in a breath so she could hold perfectly still when she had them.

ABOUT THE AUTHOR

Ellen Lesser lives in Brookfield, Vermont. She is a graduate of Yale College and of the Master of Fine Arts in Writing Program at Vermont College. Her short stories, book reviews and interviews have appeared in *The Village Voice*, *Mississippi Review*, *New England Review and Bread Loaf Quarterly*, *The Missouri Review* and other magazines. She is married to the poet Roger Weingarten. This is her first novel.